The Librarian's

Treasure

Katherine H. Brown

1

The only one of the four men without a beard had fiery red hair that seemed to crackle and undulate like real flames. Drake rubbed his eyes, thinking maybe it was time to put down the Jameson…for good. When he opened them, the movement had stopped, though the red coloring remained rich and vivid.

Wondering how he hadn't seen them before he closed the pub, Drake walked slowly around the bar. It was on the tip of his tongue to tell them to leave, but some tingling curiosity kept him from actually doing it.

The four men were short. Not your average short, no; the men's chins barely rose above the bar top. He had almost mistaken them for children. Drake leaned over the bar to take their orders. After all, he had nowhere else to go, besides the small bed in the apartment upstairs.

"We're not here for food or drink, lad," said the man on the far left, hands stuffed in his pockets. The voice was lilting, almost musical, the words said with a grin.

Drake frowned, crossing his arms. "Then what are you doing in my pub?"

Another of the men stepped forward. "Here for your help, we are." He held an ornate cane loosely in his grasp, tapping it on Drake's chest as he spoke.

"Listen, I don't know what you want, but I think you should leave." Drake calculated the odds of being able to throw all four of the men out at the same time. The redhead looked like he might still be trouble, short or not.

The last man on the right flicked his wrist, and a drawstring bag clinked heavily onto the bar in front of Drake, who could have sworn it simply dropped from nowhere. He hadn't seen the man holding a bag, nor had he had time to pull it from his pocket. Drake shook his head to clear his crazy imaginings. He opened the bag warily, and gold coins spilled out.

How many Euros would this much gold be?

"Help we need. Gold we have." The man with the cane thumped it on the floor, and another bag of gold coin materialized next to the first. "Interested?"

Drake stared. The second bag definitely came out of nowhere. No question about it. He thought he should tell the strange men to leave, to take their tricks and their gold and get out of his pub. He palmed a few of the coins, rolling the cold metal between his fingers.

Unable to help himself, he said, "I'm listening."

The curly red hair of the beardless man crackled and danced again. The man with the cane, the leader, nodded to the second man who began a fantastic tale, the air itself seeming to swell and hum along with his melodious speech.

2.

Drake watched her. The woman didn't even know he was there, following her every move with his eyes.

She's back. Again. Serious doubts snaked their way into Drake's mind, doubts that she could be the woman he had been sent to find, doubts that anyone else could be a less likely mark. In fact, he doubted whether he should have listened to those odd little men and come at all. He'd been watching her for weeks as he staked out the building, and she seemed so very…ordinary…plain really, even if he were to be kind with his assessment of her.

Slightly below average height, hair piled precariously in a knot at the top of her head. It appeared to be a dark shade of brown, but as Drake never observed her wearing it down, he couldn't tell for certain. Watching grew dull. Time was of the essence, or so he'd been told. It seemed as if he might have been sent on a wild goose chase, for there was surely nothing special about that woman.

"Oh!" The woman, slightly startled, took a step back.

Finally! He had her attention at last. Much to Drake's frustration, it had taken nearly knocking her down, of all things, to get that attention. He had been trying all week to catch her eye as she visited the library each day, wandering, browsing the floor to ceiling shelves thoroughly before ever selecting a thing, carrying around stacks of books, keeping some and shelving others, searching the card catalog while chewing on her bottom lip, making notes on scraps of paper as she poured through the towers of books beside her. No matter what, she only had eyes for the books.

*　　　　*　　　　*

Drake's first attempt had been Tuesday. Abysmal weather worked against him, however, driving hordes of people to seek out the warm lighting, the almost-plush couches, and coffee, tepid at best, from the library's Corner Café.

Corner Café. A laughable moniker indeed, had he been in a laughing mood. The barely three-by-four-foot area of seating curved around the counter where an aged employee of the library chose to spend her days serving up poor coffee and even poorer gossip in between checking out books to patrons. It did not deserve the lofty title of Café.

Needless to say, posing as the charming and intellectual student studying in the library did not attract the woman's attention, not with so many others crowding around, complaining loudly about the weather. No, she avoided people it seemed, so Tuesday had been another waste of his time.

Wednesday, there was no opportunity to engage since the monthly report was scheduled. And wasn't that a fun time. Drake reported exactly what he had observed, as well as his thoughts on that fool's errand, only to be dismissed, told once again that she was the key, that they depended on him to determine how much she knew, counted on him to get her to Ireland even.

Thursday, he tried again. Drake took to the shelves, appearing to read titles while skimming the library for her presence. He felt her before he saw her. Over the previous agonizingly long month of watching, Drake became attuned to her. It was like an exhalation or a sigh when she entered, as if the library itself had been holding its breath in anticipation. As she began her circuitous route amongst the rows, hands skimming the shelves, he endeavored to place himself in her path. Each time he did, she sidestepped him, never looking up, taking no heed of his five-nine muscular frame occupying more than half the aisle. It was as if he wasn't there. Time and again, Drake managed to guess the correct row and be there when she approached, only to be strolled by without a spare glance. After more than fifteen frustrating minutes spent in such an exasperating dance, he gave up before she became suspicious.

Friday. It must be Friday, Drake decided. He spent most of Thursday evening debating and deciding how to bring about a meeting, and finally, his plan had succeeded.

Somewhat.

*   *   *

"So sorry about that," Drake apologized, only a small lilt of his Irish accent remaining, mostly wiped away by years in English boarding schools and college. He looked down at the woman and saw her focus was not on him, but on the box of old books he carried.

So much for gaining her attention, Drake thought in frustration. He forced himself to smile.

3.

I didn't even see you there." A voice interrupted Raegan's perusal of the dusty old books dumped at her feet. "Are you okay?"

"Hmm?" she murmured, eyes scanning the books. "Oh, yes. Yes, I'm fine." She pulled her gaze upward to the man she had clumsily run into. She was a bit disappointed in herself; she usually avoided people better than that. "My fault for not looking where I was going." Raegan froze upon finding the most intense amber eyes she had ever seen looking back at her.

Great, she chided herself internally, *just great. First you try to run this guy over, and now, you're staring like an idiot. Come on, Rae, pull it together*. However, before she could gather her wits and prove to herself that she was still capable of speech, the man in front of her spoke.

"No problem at all."

He looked as if he were going to say more.

"Ok then, I'll get out of your way." Raegan tried to quickly escape down the end of the aisle, past the unsettlingly handsome stranger. Unfortunately for her, he chose just that moment to shift the box in his arms, and she collided with the corner, overturning it once again.

"Sheesh." Raegan groaned and dropped to her knees, carefully straightening the books that had scattered at their feet. "I'm so sorry." The words tumbled quickly from her mouth.

He bent to help clean up the mess. "I think this one is on me," he joked. "I'm Drake, by the way."

"Rae. Well, Raegan actually," she forced herself to reply. "I hope I didn't damage any of your books."

As she methodically stacked the volumes, Raegan scanned the titles and was surprised at the subject matter. The guy, with his noticeably muscled chest and thick arms, struck her as the type to be hitting the gym, not cracking open books on leadership and self-help topics. She quirked an eyebrow and raised *Command Your Own Destiny* out of the pile to look at it closer, but Drake quickly snatched it away.

"Not my books," Drake corrected her. "I'm stacking them for the library, actually. I just took a part-time position here."

Raegan went very still.

"Oh." She managed the word in such a way that it wasn't clear whether she meant it as a question or a statement.

"How about you?" Drake questioned. "Come here often?"

"Yes, somewhat often." Raegan chewed on her bottom lip, clearly preoccupied again. She placed the last of the books into the box and quickly stood. "Well, there you go. I've got to run," she stammered.

4.

A *part-time job. What was I thinking?
I'm not cut out for this sneaking
around, clandestine business
anymore. I've been out of the game too long.*
Drake placed his head in his hands,
replaying the earlier conversation, if it could
even be called a conversation. Raegan was
nothing like any female he had ever met.

First of all, he'd never had to work to
get attention. Usually, there was more
attention than he wanted. Especially when
the women in question were constantly
chattering on and on about the latest this or
that and expecting him to care.

Raegan, on the other hand, almost
required surgical instruments to get her
mouth open and moving, unless it was an

apology of course. He still thought the group of men interested in her, the League, were wrong. All of them telling him that girl was important. How such a timid creature could be expected to save the village, or save it from what even, Drake still didn't understand. Back to the job though. He would simply have to talk to old Ms. Jensen at the Corner Café about a part-time position or a period of volunteer work.

*   *   *

"What do you mean you can't even authorize me to volunteer?" Drake asked impatiently on Monday.

Hand on her hip, Ms. Evelyn Jensen shrugged. "Just what I said. I'm not in charge. You'll have to ask the owner."

"The owner? But this is a public library? Isn't it owned by the city or something?" Drake asked, dragging a hand through his shaggy brown hair.

"Public library, private ownership. Ask the owner, like I told you. I'm sure she could use a man just like you." Her gaze raked him up and down, and a slight twinkle came to her eye.

"Fine," Drake gave in. "Could you tell me where to find the owner?"

Ms. Jensen smiled and turned back to her coffee pot, nabbing it to pour another cup for the older gentleman approaching. "Don't you worry. She's not hard to find. Comes in almost every day in fact."

Drake thought back through the faces he had seen coming and going from the library the previous few months. He tried to place one that was a constant. Nobody stood out, none other than…

Surely not!

Nobody else came to mind though, so Drake sat down to wait, all the while hoping he was wrong.

She was later than usual, but when she finally arrived, Drake sensed a difference in her before he turned her direction. Of course, it didn't take a genius to see that she was heading straight for him.

Or to tell that she was angry.

"Listen," she began in a voice barely contained to what Drake considered a normal library level. "I don't know who you are or what you are doing here, but you need to leave."

"I—" Drake started to stand up, but she cut him off.

"No, I don't know why you would lie, but I know you don't work at this library, so don't try to argue. Just go!" Raegan pointed towards the door.

"Raegan," Drake remained seated as he spoke quietly. "Give me a moment to explain." He didn't think she would buy the next bit, but had to give it a try. No matter what, he needed to complete his assignment for the League. Oddly, he found he wanted to know if they were right or wrong about Raegan being their long-awaited savior. And if nothing else, he had to finish the assignment to receive the rest of his payment.

Raegan crossed her arms and lifted one eyebrow. She glanced meaningfully at her watch and back to him.

Drake blew out a breath and spoke. The words he'd rehearsed flowing easily. "I'm new in town. I've been coming to the library for a little while and couldn't help but notice you." Drake left out the *especially since I've been sent to spy on you and possibly accompany you to another country* comment that drifted sarcastically through his mind. "It seemed like getting a job at the library would be a good way to get to know you."

Both of Raegan's eyebrows were raised and her lips pursed. Her facial expressions made it obvious she didn't like the sound of his story. She probably pictured him as a lunatic stalker or something equally terrible. Drake watched Raegan crossing and uncrossing her arms in front of her chest, could sense her building up to another dismissal of him, so he kept speaking, faster that time.

"I also thought Ms. Jensen ran the place alone and would be happy to have my help. I planned to ask her for a job today. Of course, much to my surprise, she insisted I needed to speak to the owner. Apparently, that is you?" He let the question linger a moment before launching into his last shot at selling her need to keep him in the library. "There seem to be a few rooms with light bulbs needing replacement. Surely, having an extra hand around to climb ladders do the heavy lifting couldn't hurt?"

"I still don't think…" Before Rae could finish, there was a not-so-subtle throat clearing from her left.

Ms. Jensen shuffled toward them.

"Now, Raegan, I hate to admit it, but this fellow is right about there being things he could do around here." Evie Jensen held up a hand to prevent interruption. "Ever since my dear Earl passed on, things have been slipping, and we haven't gotten a new maintenance man yet. I'm not as young as I used to be, and boxes seem to be getting heavier every day."

"Please," Drake asked humbly, bringing Raegan's attention back to him. He held her gaze. "I'd be happy to help."

*   *   *

Raegan had listened to Drake's fervent speech, feeling nothing more than annoyance and a little trepidation. Evie's comment gave her pause, however.

Not wanting to look away first, Raegan stared back at Drake for a few seconds before she finally tossed her arms to her side and gave her head a little shake, causing a few strands of her hair to escape from the bun at the top of her head. Subconsciously brushing at the loose pieces of hair, Rae considered her next words carefully. She cringed with guilt inside.

Have I really been making things hard for Evie by not getting extra help before now? Has my precious library suffered from my reluctance to hire someone new? she wondered.

Raegan sighed. "Come in tomorrow at 8:00 a.m., before the library opens. After an interview, if I agree with Ms. Jensen's assessment that you could be useful, we will discuss the terms of your employment, Mister…" She let the sentence trail as she waited for Drake to provide his surname.

Drake, looking relieved, held out a hand. "Fletcher."

Raegan briefly shook his hand, then turned abruptly and left the library.

*   *   *

Tuesday morning, Drake arose early and set about his morning routine automatically, mentally preparing to take on Raegan again, convinced she would have changed her mind. He could tell she wasn't happy with being cajoled into hiring him by Ms. Jensen. And speaking of Ms. Jensen, wasn't she an odd duck? He couldn't quite figure her out, but he had no doubt thanks were owed to her for pulling him out of the fire the day before.

He reached into the mini fridge in the small loft kitchen and snagged an apple. While the apple wasn't nearly as delicious as the carrageen moss pudding with raspberries that he preferred, it temporarily satisfied his sweet tooth. Drake ambled to the closet and considered his next move, working at a library. That, of course, assumed he could convince Raegan to hire him against her better judgement.

And he better convince her. There were only three weeks before another report was due.

He picked up a pair of dark-wash jeans from the shelf, stepped into them, and turned to find a shirt. Black t-shirt in hand, Drake went back to the kitchen, taking another bite from his apple and straddling a bar stool to look out the window. The library was right across the street of his rented loft apartment. Directly in his sight were broad stone steps leading up to the library's double wooden doors, doors which were carved with scenes of assorted fictional characters and species.

With the sun barely beginning to rise to roof-top level, he knew there were a few more minutes before he needed to leave for his meeting. He hoped the new library job would give him an opportunity to get information out of Raegan about her past. There was nothing anywhere he researched that indicated she was indeed the woman he was sent to find, but there was also nothing to contradict it. Basically, there was nothing about her anywhere.

Drake was determined to know for certain by his next report and be on a plane home to his pub in the quiet country. The city, full of buildings and pavement, was wearisome.

*　　　　*　　　　*

Drake entered the antiquated library and looked around for any sign of Raegan before glancing down at his watch. Since he was about five minutes early, he made his way to Ms. Jensen at her usual station in the Corner Café. "Thank you," he said as he leaned up against the counter.

"Don't be thanking me yet." Ms. Jensen smirked as she looked up from reading her cozy mystery novel, *Rest, Relax,*

Run for Your Life. "I plan to see that you work hard around here, Mr. Fletcher, was it?"

"Yes, Drake Fletcher. And I am happy to be of service, madam," Drake responded with a smirk of his own and a nod of his head. Before he could find out just what work Ms. Jensen had planned for him, the library door opened. Drake turned slowly to face the entrance and caught his breath.

Raegan had arrived.

He watched her come through the ornate double doors as he had so many other times. That day, however, was different. She seemed different. Drake couldn't quite place why, maybe the set of her shoulders? The confident stride, perhaps? It was just a sense he had of a change.

"Good morning, Raegan."

"You may call me Miss Sheridan, if you please, Mr. Fletcher," Raegan responded formally. "Good morning, Evie." Her face brightened ever so slightly as she acknowledged Ms. Jensen, and then it returned to a professional mask. "My office is this way. We will discuss your part-time job here at the library, following your interview."

With that, she rounded the counter and made an immediate left. She climbed a two-tiered staircase that stood well-obscured by a bookshelf containing volumes on various types of soils.

Drake followed.

Upon arriving at the top of the staircase, another ornate door met them; however, that one gave him pause. He slowed to study the depictions of a magnificent forest scene with small fairies and what he recognized from folklore as sprites flitting among the flora. Realizing Raegan had preceded him into the office, he shifted his gaze away and entered the room.

As she unwound her scarf and placed her knitted headband on the hat rack by the door, Drake realized one thing that was different about Raegan.

Her hair.

It was flowing straight down her back, rather than in the haphazard knot of a bun she usually wore. As she turned to face him, her hair caught the sunlight from the row of windows situated around a long window-seat at the rear of the office.

Drake realized something else, that he had been wrong on two counts about Raegan Sheridan.

First, rather than a dark brown, her hair held shades of both brown and the deepest tinges of red, all interspersed. It fell in fiery waves below her shoulder blades. The second thing he knew he had been wrong about was his assessment of Raegan as plain. He stared at her as he waited for her to decide his fate and found her to be undeniably striking. It was at that point that he began to worry that, in all of the weeks of watching Raegan Sheridan, maybe he hadn't been paying any attention at all.

He gave his scrambled brain a small shake and scanned her office, her inner sanctum, surmising a few more things about Raegan. Comfort and whimsy were evidently as important to her as organization. A desk was five or six feet from the door and drew the eye based on quality, craftsmanship, and unique coloring, the legs layers of multiple types of wood bringing light, dark, and even reddish-brown hues to the picture. The desktop was solid round and magnificent. It appeared to be a cross-section of a large redwood tree that had been at least seventy years old, judging by the rings visible.

A filing cabinet, partially concealed to the right behind the coat rack, was painted a daisy-yellow but showed meticulous labeling and no loose papers in sight. The two trays on a small table to the left of the cabinet held nothing in either inbox or outbox, evidence that paperwork was dealt with quickly and completely.

Not to be ignored, the chairs in the office were as unique as the desk, but it was there that the touch of whimsy manifested.

Three toadstools, or mushrooms, about two feet tall and carved from separate wooden pieces, were clustered on the visitor side of the desk, cushioned on the tops. To the left of the room, opposite the file cabinet and coat rack, was a lounge-chair that was anything but ordinary. Wide at the top, it sloped gently down to a point and was the perfect picture of a giant leaf, wrought completely from metal and painted a deep forest green.

Choosing the middle mushroom more than a little reluctantly, Drake seated himself directly across from the winged chair behind the desk in which Raegan positioned herself. And winged was a literal description, not the style of chair. Reagan Sheridan currently sat on, or in—he wasn't certain which—a chair made of the same metal as the leaf lounge but shaped like a massive butterfly. Two turquoise wings spanning three or four feet made the small woman seem more diminutive and yet oddly mystical, almost faerie even.

"A beautiful office, Miss Sheridan," Drake commented, realizing she sat patiently, waiting for him to finish examining the room.

Raegan folded her hands together atop the desk. "Thank you. About your position, um, job here at the library, have you brought a resume or work history of any kind?"

"I'm sorry. After we spoke yesterday, I was unaware either would be needed. I'm afraid I'm a little short on references at the moment, but I'm used to heavy work and handling things. Anything that your regular maintenance personnel would have done, just give me a list and it'll be taken care of." He hoped she wouldn't argue with him when he had just offered to do any and everything that they could need around there, carte blanche. If that didn't earn him a job, he didn't know what would.

"I see." Raegan unclasped her hands and reached into a drawer near the top of the desk, retrieving a manila folder, pulling free a sheet of paper. She turned it around so that it was face-up toward Drake and held it forward to him.

Drake took the paper and skimmed through what appeared to be a standard, though slightly thin, "Application for Hire" form. Evidently, Raegan wasn't planning to make it simple at all. He wondered how soon she needed the form, pondered what exactly he could give for information when none of it would be verifiable.

Drake looked back up to find Raegan studying him. Quickly, she glanced away and gestured to a small tree figurine on his side of the desk. It was then he noticed the tree was hollow and contained several pens and pencils. It seemed *immediately* was the answer to his concern about when the paperwork was required.

Raegan seemed determined to show power in that particular instance, so Drake chose to pick up a dark blue pen. Not wishing to fill out the form sitting on a mushroom and being under a microscope, however, he braved the silence with a question, hoping that he could rattle the new business-like woman in front of him back to her normal relaxed and frazzled self. "Would you mind terribly if I were to borrow a book and fill this out at the window seat there?" He gestured behind her. Not waiting for a response, he took the pen and paper in one hand while standing up and reaching to grasp a book that was face down on the large desk.

"Excuse me," Raegan started.

"Oh, no excuse needed, Miss Sheridan. I'm sure you didn't realize how difficult it is to write perched on such an intriguing seat, but I'm afraid I may topple off at any moment." With that, he continued around the desk, past the fuming Miss Raegan Sheridan, and seated himself comfortably in the center window seat. He leaned against one of the corner frames and proceeded to fill out the application.

Date, name, ability to lift more than forty pounds. The form was nothing out of the ordinary and blessedly short. Other than a few questions he preferred not to answer in full and answers he knew she wouldn't accept without more questions, such as the one concerning his previous occupations and reasons he left, Drake had it filled out in no time.

Drake let out a sigh and was about to make his way back to the desk where Raegan had begun tapping her foot impatiently when suddenly a loud crash came from downstairs.

Raegan swung her eyes to him for a split second before springing from her chair and making her way around the massive desk. Drake exhaled gratefully for whatever distraction had bought him more time, folded the paper furtively, and stuck it deep into his jeans pocket before quickly making his way after Raegan down the staircase.

"Oh! Evie, are you okay?" Raegan supported Ms. Jensen by the arm in the small room behind the Corner Café, the entrance directly across from the staircase to Raegan's office.

Ms. Jensen shrugged off the assistance and massaged her left hip with a small movement of her hand. "Yes, I'm just fine dear. Only managed to stumble into the crate of coffee there when I came in, and the bulb went out. Startled me some, it did."

"We heard such a loud crash," Drake mentioned.

Ms. Jensen looked into the room and turned back to the two of them, waiving off their concern again. "I managed to knock over not only the coffee crate in the dark but then grabbed for my balance and bumped about seven of the round, blue tins of biscuits and several more boxes of cookies that were on the shelf next to it. Those of course fell off the shelf into the mop and broom, which came clattering down as well."

Raegan slowly massaged her temples.

"Don't worry about it, dear." Ms. Jensen patted her shoulder. "Seeing that we have this strapping maintenance man here, he can clean and organize it all to rights in minutes as his first assignment." She gestured to Drake.

"I suppose so but…" Raegan stopped and looked at Drake when she saw Evie rub her hip again. "But as soon as that is finished, I want you on a ladder replacing all of the other burnt-out bulbs in the library."

Drake knew only the apparent pain and exhaustion of Ms. Jensen had made Raegan soften and give him the job. She obviously would do anything for the woman, which meant Drake needed to start ingratiating himself with her right away. "Yes, Miss Sheridan." He made sure to enunciate slowly and clearly, happy to see a slight flush of embarrassment heat Raegan's face in return. "And I thank you for this opportunity."

He chuckled to himself. He could play the subservient if needed.

Interview concluded, Drake headed immediately into the storage room and started to work. He stacked cans of unspilled coffee in one area, and open cans whose contents were emptied all over the room during the fall went into boxes to be thrown out. Manual labor, he was more accustomed

to that than the lying and spying required of
him those days.

5.

For two weeks, Drake labored under the stern taskmaster, Evelyn Jensen. There was not a light fixture in the entire twenty-two-hundred-square-foot library that had a single burnt-out bulb any longer. Boxes and crates had been unpacked in the storage room that doubled as a pantry, and all of the shelves were neatly arranged. Those had been re-done twice as there was an intense debate betwixt Ms. Jensen and him whether the foodstuffs should be arranged categorically or alphabetically. Old rugs had been rolled up and taken out to have years of dust beaten from them, though Drake was unsure he would ever again get said dust out of his eyes and nostrils.

Floors had been mopped until they shone and reflected lights back toward the ceiling. It was twice as bright in the library foyer as Drake had ever seen it. Raegan kept herself scarce during that entire period, rarely darkening the door of the library. When she did, it was with the constant habit of disappearing quickly into her sanctuary upstairs with the unmistakable sound of a closing door to dissuade entry or disturbance of any kind.

It was also during that two-week period that Drake had gotten to know Evie—as she insisted that he call her—and began ferreting out more small bits of Raegan's history, though not as much as he would have liked. Raegan was an orphan; her parents died when she was a child according to Evie, first the mother when she was an infant and her father when she was only twelve. Raegan herself was born in a small English hamlet, though it seemed obvious there was some Irish background to her heritage—her father's side, Evie said. When it was that her parents made the move to England, she had no idea, much less the why of the matter, and Evie wasn't sure if Raegan even knew.

When he asked how Raegan came to own the library, the older woman just shrugged. "It's always been Raegan's, of course." Nothing in the bare details he uncovered proved or disproved the question of Raegan's identity as it mattered to Drake, and with only a week left before he was expected to report in, it was time to push Raegan Sheridan for the answers she alone could provide.

Drake wiped his palms on his faded jeans, closed the lid to the dumpster in the alleyway where he had been taking out the garbage, and re-entered the library. He stopped to look around and had to admit to himself that the library appeared to be a whole new place with all of the cleaning and minor repairs that Evie had set before him.

Finally, however, she had declared that it was up to Raegan which duties were next on his agenda, just the excuse he needed to seek out the elusive woman. Suspecting the ever-distant *Miss Sheridan* would be unhappy about his intrusion, he snatched three thumbprint cookies and a small plate, winking at Evie on his way past, and made his way to the staircase behind the Corner Café. Drake had already prepared a mental list of a number of larger repairs that needed to be made: two of the east windows needed repair, a mirror in the women's restroom needed replacing, and more than a few shutters outside hung in disrepair and in want of new paint. With ammunition at the ready in case Raegan was hoping to call a halt to his part-time job, Drake was confident he would be able to continue in the role. He did not fool himself into thinking a few cookies would sweeten her attitude towards him enough to get the answers he needed, though.

At the top of the stairs, Drake again couldn't help but lean in to look closer at the scene playing out on the wooden door. The fairies and sprites seemed to exist in harmony, a few flying through the air as if in a merry chase. Two fairies, a male and female, in a pool of water looked put out by a sprite splashing droplets of water towards them with a glint of mischief in his eye. Flowers were numerous and the petals overly large. A family of hedgehogs traveled in the background, and one hare could be seen at the very edge of the door, drinking just before the pond ended. And there, at the edge of the pond, stood a short little man that Drake hadn't noticed before beside what looked to be a pot of gold.

Quite suddenly, the door opened, and Drake was standing within inches of Raegan Sheridan, his nose almost brushing her shoulder due to his intense study of the door which had pulled him in for a closer look. Straightening, Drake took a half-step back, not before inhaling the heady scent of wild rose emanating from Raegan.

For her part, Raegan didn't look nearly as shocked, which meant she must have heard him coming up the stairs. She did, however, raise both eyebrows in question at finding him stooping at her door.

"Peering in keyholes, Mr. Fletcher?" Raegan asked, but Drake couldn't tell if she was angry or amused.

He adopted a self-deprecating grin and shook his head. "Not at all. You did catch me admiring the artwork on your office door, however. It was carved by the same individual as the main entrance doors, was it not?"

Raegan placed a hand over her heart, briefly closing her eyes, and then stepped back to allow him inside. "Yes, the same man carved each door by hand. It took several years."

"May I ask who the artisan was? I find it remarkable that he made the scenes so lifelike that one is really just waiting for them to flit right off the door and through the library." Drake watched her closely, waiting for an answer.

Raegan turned away, seemingly lost in thought, staring toward the expanse of sky outside of the windows. "The artisan, as you call him, was Brian Sheridan, my dad."

Momentarily shocked, Drake stood and stared at Raegan. Her father had masterfully portrayed the essence of the tiny magical beings on the doors? He wouldn't have guessed. Maybe there was a possibility of more to her past than he thought. Perhaps he was there on more than just a fool's assignment or following the ramblings of an eccentric band of men.

Drake regained his thoughts and looked down at the plate of cookies he still held. Raegan seemed to have forgotten his presence; she stared out the windows, fingering a leather strap at her neck.

I am always trying to gain this woman's attention, Drake thought wryly. He walked with slow but deliberate steps so as not to startle her, moving to Raegan's side and softly touching her upper arm, extending the plate of cookies before her with his other hand. "Your father must have been quite a talented man. I brought you some thumbprint cookies, Miss Sheridan. Evie tells me they are your favorite, though, I've never tried one myself."

"Thank you," Raegan replied automatically. She inhaled deeply and took the plate of cookies before making her way not to the desk as Drake had expected, but to the large window seat instead. "Please, join me, Mr. Fletcher. Evie does make the best thumbprint cookies this side of the ocean, and I insist you have a taste. These appear to have raspberry jam in the center today, a treat indeed."

Drake sat in the corner opposite Raegan, the cookie plate on the center cushion between them. Reaching forward, he lifted the top cookie to his mouth and looked towards her while taking the first bite. He knew she was watching for his reaction to the cookie, but he flattered himself that her stare remained transfixed as he licked raspberry jam from his upper lip. For a split second, her pupils dilated, and Drake felt his chest tighten. Raegan flicked her eyes upward, meeting his. He held her gaze as she studied him.

Perhaps Miss Sheridan wasn't as resistant to him as she'd led him to believe. Excitement stirred at the thought until he tamped it down. He had a job to do. In and out. Bring Raegan to the League, and get back to his pub. He didn't need anything else.

"Delicious," Drake declared, breaking the moment. "You were right. These are great cookies." With that, he tossed the other half into his mouth to finish off.

Raegan picked up a cookie of her own, smiling as she nibbled off several small bites. She finished the thumbprint cookie and dusted the crumbs from her lap. She took the plate containing the last cookie to her desk, sat down in the butterfly chair, and gestured for Drake to join her.

Drake waited as Raegan regained her composure, deciding it best to broach the subject of why he had come. "Evie says that I should find out from you what my next priorities are to be for work. It seems she can't think of another thing in the library for me to spit-shine or polish." He grinned jokingly.

"Evie, is it?" Raegan questioned, both eyebrows raised. "I take it you two are getting on famously then." It came out as a statement rather than a question, so Drake made no reply.

She sighed. "Evie says you have been a blessing, and that the library hasn't *gleamed* this much in ages. I guess I have been neglectful in the past few years, much to my shame. If you are willing to continue on as our maintenance man, I would be an idiot to refuse you."

"I thank you for the compliments, Miss Sheridan. I would be happy to continue working for you." Drake paused before continuing. "I do have some pressing business to attend next week and wonder would it be acceptable if I take next Tuesday, Wednesday, and Thursday off from work?"

"That will be fine, Mr. Fletcher, and," she paused and took a deep breath, "I'd be happy if you called me Raegan."

"My pleasure, Raegan." His Irish brogue, which had been slipping from his lips more often, made its way forth to caress her name. "But only if you will call me Drake. Is it a deal?" He raised an eyebrow and waited, smiling.

"Deal." Reagan rolled her eyes. "I believe we should move on to discuss what projects you will need to complete for the library next."

*   *   *

The next couple of days passed easily enough. Thursday found Drake on rickety scaffolding two stories high as he took advantage of a rare day with no rain pouring from the few clouds floating past outside.

It turned out Raegan was just as difficult a taskmaster as Evie. It was not enough that he made the necessary repairs to the windows whose glass was cracked and put the shutters hanging askew to rights. No, she had decided every window needed a good scrubbing, and when that was over, a fresh coat of paint in a new color was to be put on each shutter. Drake counted; he was on the twelfth shutter of the morning, possibly covered in more forest green paint than the other eleven shutters combined.

He placed the paint brush on a tray beside the five-gallon paint bucket, replaced the lid, and stood up to stretch. Drake spared a glance at his watch, seeing it was almost twelve-thirty, and decided lunch was in order. Not that he was particularly hungry, thanks to the continual smell of paint as he worked, but if he didn't have a break soon, he might have forgotten what he was about and start to paint the whole building green. He strode briskly to the edge of the scaffolding as if he wasn't three stories above ground and swung himself lithely over the edge onto the second rung of the ladder.

Drake reached the pavement at the bottom, dusted off his hands, and turned toward the entrance. At that very moment, the large doors swung open, and Raegan exited the building. She was rummaging in her purse with her head down, and Drake smiled to himself.

It was going to be easier than he thought.

He took a small step to the side and caught Raegan by the arm as she nearly smacked into him. "Raegan, what a pleasant surprise." Drake grinned as he held on a moment more than necessary and then released her.

"Oh, good afternoon." Raegan nodded. "I'm just on my way to lunch." She tried to step around him.

"Lunch sounds incredible. I think I'll join you. I've worked up quite an appetite. Are the shutters to your liking?" He gestured upward past the tall scaffolding to the six sparkling windows, each with two glossy shutters framing them, brightly reflecting the sun.

"Yes, absolutely!" Raegan smiled looking up at his most recent handiwork.

"Excellent. So where are we lunching?" Drake responded before Raegan could correct his assumption that she was agreeing to his inviting himself to lunch.

6.

Half an hour later, they sat across from one another at a cozy corner booth in a small pub called The Red Deer. Drake had taken time to scrub as clean as he could manage in the library bathroom sink and changed into a fresh shirt.

Judging by the table legs propped on stones to take out the wobble, seats in desperate need of reupholstering, and a complete lack of menus, Drake assumed only locals darkened the door of the place. He sniffed and was surprised to find it smelled rather good, like food and a hint of rain. Most pubs—and he was quite familiar with more than the one he owned—smelled like stale ale at best. Some of the seedier ones smelled significantly worse.

"Nice place," he said.

Raegan nodded. "I love it."

Drake's jaw dropped in surprise when a gray-bearded man with a fisherman's cap strolled over to their booth and scooped Raegan up into a giant bear hug.

"Rae, me lass."

"Lorcan, it's so good to see you." Rae hugged the man back and then waved to Drake. "This is Drake Fletcher."

Drake prided himself on a great grip and firm handshake, but when Lorcan shook his hand, he felt as if the man were trying to grind his bones to powder. And based on the look Lorcan was shooting him, Drake's guess probably wasn't far off. The men stared each other down until Raegan laughed.

"Come on, Lorcan, give him his hand back. He can't very well be a decent maintenance man for me at the library if you break all his fingers."

Lorcan relaxed. "Helping at the library? Well, welcome. Never understood books, but our Rae loves them. So did her Da."

Drake nodded, the familiar heavy Irish accent sending him a million miles away in his thoughts. *So, Raegan did have Irish connections. That was one more point in favor of the League saying she was the woman they needed.* Raegan's voice drew him back to the dingy pub.

"We're here for lunch. Can you send out the special?"

Lorcan rubbed his hands together. "You got it."

"Colorful fellow." Drake raised his eyebrows.

"He was a friend of my dad's. I've known him since I was tiny." She faltered, sadness stealing over her features. "He and his wife took me in when my dad passed." Visibly rallying herself, Raegan smiled again, her gaze wandering to the door to the kitchen where Lorcan had disappeared. "If I don't stop by often enough for food, he and Joan assume I'm starving and show up with a week's worth of meals."

"What's the special?"

Raegan shrugged. "No idea. They change it frequently."

Drake frowned.

"Don't worry," Raegan winked. "It'll be good. Everything Lorcan cooks is good."

"Lorcan?" Drake was surprised. He couldn't picture the beast of a man behind a stove. "He does the cooking, not his wife?"

"That's right. Bless her heart, Joan can't cook a thing without burning it." Raegan shook her head, smiling fondly. "She does the accounting and inventory, ordering, business things like that."

They slid into silence, and minutes later, Lorcan reappeared, that time bearing a tray of tantalizingly fragrant bowls and steaming bread.

"Me own Irish beef stew," he said proudly.

"Is that your homemade soda bread?" Raegan rubbed her hands together.

"Would I serve ye anything else?"

Raegan dug in unceremoniously, tearing off a thick piece of bread and dragging it through her stew. "Delicious!" she exclaimed around a mouthful.

"Thank you," Drake said.

Lorcan slapped him on the back hard enough to make him wince. "A friend of Rae's is a friend of mine. The same be true about an enemy." With a fierce smile, the man disappeared back behind the bar.

Raegan continued eating, either ignoring or not noticing the subtle threat— Drake wasn't sure which. He got the impression that if he wanted any of that bread, he better grab it while he had the chance, though. Ripping off a piece, he used it as a spoon to shovel a large portion of stew into his mouth.

Well, Raegan was right.

Delicious.

He hadn't had stew that good since his mother was alive.

*   *   *

"Well," Raegan said as they walked back to the library after their hearty lunch, "Lorcan likes you."

Drake snorted. "I don't think so. The man barely tolerated me."

"Exactly. He didn't throw you out on the street or put you in the hospital. Trust me, that's high praise in the actions of Lorcan."

"He does seem very protective of you. I'd hate to see what he did when you introduced him to any of your boyfriends." Drake chuckled at the thought. "Has he sent any poor guys running and crying yet?"

Raegan ducked her head so that Drake wouldn't see her blush. "He hasn't met any."

"Smart."

"No, I mean, I haven't had any boyfriends." Raegan blew out a ragged breath. "I've really avoided people since losing my parents. Being close to people, it scares me."

Drake nodded. "I can appreciate that. I lost my dad just a year ago. I can't imagine losing my family as a child like you."

Raegan tucked a strand of hair behind her ear. She looked up when they were nearly back to the library. "Well, I've got work to do since lunch took longer than expected. Let Evie know when you finish the shutters, please." With that, she climbed the steps and disappeared into the safe, familiar walls.

7.

Drake arrived tired, hungry, and frustrated at the small fountain in the garden behind The Brazen Beast, a small but popular pub in Dublin. He'd walked over an hour to Liverpool, ridden seven and a half hours on the ferry, and to make things worse, he had to do it all again day after the next to return to the library. He wanted a good meal and a bed so he could be well-rested before checking how his own pub was faring in his absence. His stomach growled as he recalled a particularly delicious bowl of stew, and he smiled as he thought over the easy conversation he and Raegan shared that day.

"Happy enough to have already found the treasure you look, lad."

Drake turned to the voice at his right and found two of the four men from the League of Leprechauns seated on a low wall around the garden. How they had climbed up there without so much as a sound, he didn't know. "I'm still not convinced there is a treasure," he admitted to Ronan and Brandon. At least, he believed those were their names. He had the hardest time telling the small men apart.

"This doubt you have, why exactly?"

Their speech pattern was almost as confusing as their names. That time, the voice came from behind and to his left. Drake spun, not surprised to find the other two members of the League. He was certain the man with the fiery red hair was called Aiden. The other might have been Oran. Drake shook his head. It didn't really matter who was who.

"If there is a lost treasure, I doubt Raegan Sheridan has it. The library she owns isn't flashy. In fact, parts were barely clean before I got there."

"Perhaps Princess Raegan the treasure hasn't found," the main spokesman—Ronan it must have been then—tapped his chin, fingers flexing around his cane. "First, she will need the key."

The other three murmured assent.

That was the other thing about the odd group of men that got under Drake's skin. They kept referring to Raegan as a princess. From the moment they approached him in his pub, pulled him out of his ale, and offered enough gold to pay off his father's debts, they had been determined that he find the *lost princess* and bring her home to Kivarleigh. What she was supposed to be princess of, they hadn't told him so far.

"What key?" Drake asked, his irritation growing. "What does the key go to?"

"Secrets it will unlock. Know you will when you and the princess find it."

Drake crossed his arms. "No. I'm tired of this wild goose chase. Tell me something useful, something that makes sense. Why should I get back on that infernal ferry to England and try to convince Raegan to jump on a plane to Ireland if I don't even know why you want her there?"

The men shared a look, seeming to converse without words. At a nod from Ronan, Aiden spoke. "Time to come home it is. Give the princess this medallion. Her da's it was. She must come save the people."

Drake held out a hand for the medallion. The weight surprised him as he turned it over, admiring the intricate details in the metal. He wasn't sure if it was bronze or simply tarnished, but even the dark color couldn't disguise the fine lines depicting a meadow of flowers, a colorless rainbow arcing across the sky.

He looked up from his study to find the League gone, vanished into the night.

8.

Raegan noticed the lack of Evie's laughing banter early Tuesday morning. She noticed the complete silence that met her as she walked outside for lunch on Wednesday. She noticed grime building up on the windows by Wednesday night when she locked up to go home. Thursday morning, she noticed the emptiness in her chest that she'd been steadfastly ignoring.

In effect, Raegan noticed Drake's absence the whole time he was gone. It chafed her to admit that she missed him. His easy humor with Evie. His constant and annoying habit of showing up near her unexpectedly. His care for the jobs he did in the library—her library. If she were honest with herself, she simply missed him. She chastised herself, wondering when someone determined to be alone and happy had become alone and lonely instead.

Raegan gave herself a mental shake and decided to see if she could help Evie with anything the rest of the day. There were a couple of people seated in the Corner Café lounge area, and she stopped to check on them, accepting a pretend cup of tea from one adorable toddler.

"Need anything?" she asked Evie, finding her bent over, digging in cabinets behind the counter.

Evie heaved herself up, wiping sweat from her forehead. "Actually, yes. I seem to be out of Styrofoam cups. Can you be a dear and check the storage room for me?"

Raegan smiled, happy to have a task to keep herself distracted. "Absolutely! I'll be back in a minute."

Her happy bubble burst the moment she opened the door. Thoughts of Drake slammed into her from every direction. All of his work was evident, from the well-oiled and squeak-free door to the meticulously organized shelves with all of the heavy items closer to the floor, new labels on every box. She sighed. At least the cups were simple to find. She plucked a bag of them off a shelf and returned to Evie.

The remainder of the afternoon passed slowly. Evie didn't need any other help, so eventually, Raegan took herself off to check and organize shelves.

9.

Morning rays flitted through the blinds and woke Drake early Friday morning. With a stretch, he replayed his past few days in his head. His pub had been getting on well without him, better, in fact, without a moping pub owner drinking more than the customers, according to his bartender. His conversation with the League still frustrated him, and something about the medallion niggled at the back of his mind, but he couldn't figure out what was bothering him. As soon as he thought about the medallion, though, he knew he needed to get to the library and see Raegan right away.

Throwing back the sheets, Drake brushed his teeth and dressed. He ran a hand through his hair, noting that before too long he would need a haircut, and opted to skip breakfast in favor of getting to the library right away. He could always grab a snack from Evie. That woman could make a mean pastry.

The musty scent of books greeted him when he entered the library not ten minutes later. He smiled; he was beginning to associate the smell with Raegan. Evie was chatting to a young mom and pouring a cup of hot chocolate for a young child. Drake waved but didn't interrupt. He wound his way up the spiral staircase and knocked on the doors to Raegan's office.

No answer.

He knocked again.

Nothing.

Drake leaned his ear close but heard no sounds from inside. She must have been somewhere in the library, roaming and reshelving books or reading in a nook like those first few weeks when he'd been watching her. *Before my presence drove her to hide away in her office so often*, he realized, wondering how far she would go to avoid him after she heard the news he had for her.

With a sigh, he descended the stairs. He'd hoped to get the conversation over with quickly, but it looked like he would have to find her first. Evie was alone, the mom and child long gone with their chocolate and books, so he joined her behind the counter.

"Coffee?" she offered.

Drake still couldn't bring himself to drink the nasty brew there and shook his head. Since he hadn't taken time to make his own coffee, he asked for a water instead.

Evie inquired politely about his trip but, sensing he wasn't in a very talkative mood, soon left him to himself. He downed his water, the medallion heavy in his pocket.

"Do you know where Raegan is at?"

She hadn't appeared to chat with him and Evie like he'd hoped she might.

"I believe she was taking the garbage out."

Drake frowned. Raegan knew he would be back on Friday. Why wouldn't she have simply waited for him to do it?

"Thanks." He tossed his cup in the trash and headed for the back doors to the alley.

The sight that met his eyes as he stepped into the overcast alleyway made him chuckle. That chuckle earned him a solid glare, but he couldn't help it. Raegan was stooped by the dumpster, digging through the garbage bag, and trying to feed little scraps of food to a tiny calico kitten, barely bigger than a scrap itself.

"I see you're back."

"As promised." Drake nodded.

Raegan stood to retie the trash bag as the kitten nuzzled against her ankle.

Drake stepped over and took the bag. "Here. I've got that. You seem to have your hands full." He quickly tied the bag and heaved it overhead into the open dumpster.

"Thanks." Raegan picked up the tiny kitten who promptly batted at a loose curl. "Has this little girl been out here when you brought out the trash before?" She gave him an accusatory look.

Drake held up his hands. "Never seen her before." He didn't need starving animals added to his list of sins before he even got to come clean to Raegan about his true purpose in being there.

Raegan eyed him suspiciously as if she were trying to decide if he was responsible for the pitiful creature's hungry state. Then she strode right past him, cuddling the kitten all the way into the library.

Drake shook his head and followed after her. First books, then a cat. It seemed he simply couldn't compete for Raegan Sheridan's attention.

*   *   *

Raegan heard Drake ascending the spiral staircase, and the rhythmic sounding of his footsteps filled her with dread. She had left the door ajar, and he entered after a small, perfunctory knock.

As Drake closed the door behind him, Raegan's stomach knotted even tighter. After finally admitting to herself that she had been missing him, she had expected to be happy and lighthearted when he returned. The look on his face and his somber mood seemed to echo every fear her heart had of getting close to people. Drake had bad news. She could feel it to her bones.

"Can we talk?"

Those three ominous words. For a moment, Raegan considered saying no. After all, it had been phrased as a question. Instead, she gathered her courage and her furry new friend and went to sit behind her desk. She needed every shield she could have.

"What do you want to talk about?"

As he sat down, Drake's easy smile and small jokes were noticeably absent. Raegan watched as he seemed to search for the words he wanted to use, rubbing his hands down the back of his neck. At last, he raised his eyes to meet her gaze, and she braced herself. *Here it comes,* she thought. *He's leaving.*

"I lied to you about why I came here."

Raegan frowned. She knew that. She'd caught him in the lie about the part-time job right away.

As if reading her mind, or perhaps she didn't have the best poker face, Drake held up a hand. What he said next went beyond her wildest expectations.

"I'm not talking about the job. I was sent here specifically to find you."

Raegan balked. "What do you mean? Sent by who? From where?" The kitten meowed and scratched her, causing Raegan to loosen her accidental squeeze on the poor thing. She found herself eyeing the desk and being disappointed that the most dangerous thing within her reach was a paperweight. "If you hurt me, I swear Lorcan will rip you into pieces and feed you to Nessa here." She hugged the kitten closer.

"Nessa?" Drake paused. "Like the Loch Ness Monster?"

Raegan glared.

"Right. Not important."

She watched as Drake seemed to gather his thoughts. When he spoke again, he had adopted a soft, gentle tone. He told her everything: starting with his father dying, the depression he fell into with the heavy drinking, leaving his job with the Irish police, or Garda as they were called, all of the debts he couldn't pay, how—on the brink of losing his father's pub—four diminutive men had shown up and offered him money to leave Ireland and travel to England to find the girl fated to save their nearby village, only afterwards introducing themselves as the League of Leprechauns.

The more Drake talked, the less reassurance she felt. He sounded like a crazy person.

"Are you insane?" Raegan asked when it became apparent his tale was over. "Or is this some elaborate joke? I hope it's a joke, but you should know that I don't think it is very funny." Her thoughts raced as fast as her heart. Sent there to find her? Who would be looking for her? She had no family. Drake had to be making it up. Raegan couldn't for the life of her figure out why he would, though, and that scared her.

"I'm sorry. It isn't a joke." Drake leaned forward earnestly. "I need to go back to Ireland. Soon. And the League wants me to convince you to come, too. They say it is time for you to come home."

"No. I don't believe you." Nessa squirmed in her arms, and Raegan let the poor kitten down. She felt alone, vulnerable, as soon as the warm and cuddly animal left her lap. "I don't know these men. I've never been to this village...this...what did you say it was called?"

"Kivarleigh."

"Never even heard of it." Raegan hugged her arms across her chest. "Why should I believe a word that you're saying?"

Drake slapped his forehead. "I forgot. One of the men told me to give you this medallion when I told you that it was time to come home." He fished in his pocket, retrieving the heavy metal object. "Said it belonged to your father." Laying the medallion on the desk, Drake leaned back to give Raegan space, but she didn't notice.

Her eyes widened, and Raegan found herself staring at a design that took her breath away. She hadn't seen it in years, almost thirteen. She lifted the medallion, the metal tingling under her fingertips.

"It looked familiar to me," Drake was saying. "Like I've seen it somewhere. Have you?"

"What?" Raegan murmured, barely hearing him.

Drake leaned forward again. "I said, have you seen it before?"

Raegan nodded, her thumb lovingly tracing the rainbow over the meadow. "My dad, he had this exact design tattooed on his shoulder. I'd forgotten."

10.

Raegan sat unmoving in her office the rest of the morning, lost in her thoughts. Evie tried to coax her out for lunch with no luck. As she traced her fingers around and around the medallion, she allowed her memories, and her tears, to flow freely.

In her mind, she was a child again. She felt her dad's hands ruffling her hair. Saw his wide smile as she brought him pictures that she had colored mimicking the creatures he had carved into the doors of the library. Felt the pride and confusion that always welled up when he told her how proud her mother would have been of her, always with such sadness. She remembered tracing the tattoo on his shoulder, much like she traced the medallion in front of her.

"What is it?" young Raegan asked.

"Ach." Her dad pulled her into his lap. "It's a special mark of my family."

"But I don't have one." She had pouted.

"Only the men get them."

"Hmmph! That's not fair."

"Aye, child. Much unfairness this life holds."

Raegan remembered coloring the symbol on her legs and coming back to show her dad. He had made her scrub it off, telling her not to draw it anymore. He said the mark was their secret.

How long it had been since she had remembered those things! And yet, there she was, face to face with a piece of her past, if Drake was to be believed. Were those men he talked about, the League, were they her dad's family? Her family? She always thought there was no one.

*　　　　*　　　　*

"Raegan!" Drake pounded on the door. The stubborn woman had locked herself in. She wouldn't even budge for Evie after the poor woman tramped all the way up that infernal spiral staircase. "Rae! Raegan Sheridan, don't make me go get Lorcan to break down these beautiful doors."

He waited. After a minute, scuffling noises sounded. A chair scooting back. Light footsteps. Drake backed up a step from the door. As Raegan opened it, he noted her puffy eyes, red cheeks, and a glare that was becoming all-too-familiar.

"What else could you possibly need to say to me?" she asked.

"I'm sorry."

Raegan frowned. "That's it?"

"No." Drake shook his head. "But I want you to know that I am sorry. The reason I'm here is because I thought you'd want to know that I finally remembered where I saw the picture from the medallion before."

"Where?"

"Come on, I'll show you." Drake descended the first two steps of the winding staircase, giving Raegan room to make the decision for herself.

Annoyance and curiosity warred in her eyes. She seemed to make up her mind as she set her mouth in a determined line and stepped out, shutting the door behind her. Drake led the way down, breathing a sigh of relief. It was progress. Slow, painful progress. He hoped he could earn her trust back before he left, whether she went to Ireland on the League's grand errand or not.

Raegan trudged grudgingly after him, all the way to the storage room. Evie, delighted at seeing he had succeeded in bringing her out of the office, brought up the rear of the procession, bearing a plate of snickerdoodle cookies.

After hugging her friend and eating a cookie, Raegan stamped impatiently. "Well? I don't see anything. Was there a medallion like this one on the shelf? Or was this another lie to get me to come downstairs?"

"Not a lie." Drake continued moving boxes around. "I know it was back here somewhere." He cleared the top two rows of one tall, metal shelf, then tested its weight. After he removed a few more things, he grabbed the legs and scooted the shelf far enough from the wall that one or two people could squeeze behind it. He stooped and disappeared from their sight for a moment.

"Aha! Over here." Drake stepped out of the way and allowed Raegan behind the shelf. "About waist level, there seems to be more carving like your dad did on all of the doors. Only, in the center is a little inset circle, and the medallion scene is there, too."

"It's hard to see." Raegan ran her hands down the wall. "Do you have a flashlight?"

Evie set the plate of cookies down and collected a flashlight from a cabinet by the door. She handed it to Drake, who held it pointed toward the carvings for Raegan.

"Odd." Raegan knelt down on the floor, bringing the small scene to eye level. It was small, not nearly as grand as the doors to the entrance or even her office. Still, she would know her dad's handiwork anywhere. She felt along the wall, her hands tingling as they rested on the section that matched the medallion and her dad's tattoo. "It's almost as if a piece is missing. I wonder." She leaned closer to the wall.

Drake craned his neck, curious. Evie shuffled closer, nearly bumping into him. The two watched as Raegan inserted the medallion into the circle of the wall.

"How strange," she muttered. "It fits perfectly."

"What do you think it means?" Evie asked.

"I don't know." Raegan stood, leveraging one hand against the wall.

As she did so, she accidentally pushed the medallion further into the wall. A click sounded. Soft whirring noises began, slowly.

Before their eyes, the wall began to swing, opening away from the storage room.

11.

Raegan stared in wonder as the wall slowed to a stop, leaving an opening just large enough to walk through. Inky blackness stared back at her. "Pass me the flashlight," she said urgently.

"Raegan, you be careful. You don't know what's back there." Evie started in on a long lecture about sticking one's nose in bad places, creepy moving walls, broken necks on rickety stairs, a whole plethora of superstitions and worries jumbled together.

But Raegan wasn't listening.

She heard Drake's comment about letting him go first, to which she only snorted. It was her library, after all.

Flashlight securely in hand, Raegan shone it first at the floor to assure herself of safe footing. Then, as she walked forward, she shone it around and gasped. "A secret room! A whole secret room of the library."

"Watch out for rotten floorboards!" Evie called out. "And traps. Don't you always read about booby-traps in secret places?"

Drake didn't waste time with words. Instead, Raegan felt him step inside behind her to see for himself what the room held.

"Isn't it magnificent?" Raegan beamed the flashlight along all of the walls. She jumped as Drake reached past her and then heard a small click as he found the light switch. The room lit up as bright as any other.

"More books?"

Raegan frowned. "You don't have to sound so disappointed."

"Well, you didn't have to sound so excited and get a guy's hopes up for a safe filled with cash or something."

"What is it?" Evie yelled from her safe place in the middle of the storage room.

Raegan poked her head back out of the secret entrance. "Come and see." She held out a hand to her friend. "I promise, nothing in here will bite you."

Evie's gasp of appreciation as she marveled at the shelves upon shelves of books more than made up for Drake's unenthusiastic response. "Gracious! Where did all of these come from?"

Drake moved about the room, scanning the shelves. "All over the world, from what I can tell." He thumbed a volume in front of him. "Several languages, too."

"Evie, would you go lock the doors and put out the closed sign?" Raegan set the flashlight down and walked across the stone floor to join Drake. So immersed were they in the shelves of books that Raegan didn't see Evie return and strike off in her own direction until it was too late. "Watch out!"

Evie's foot tangled in a rope sticking out from under a small desk, and she fell on her bottom with a thud.

Rushing to her side, Raegan grabbed Evie's hands. "Are you alright? Do you need me to get a doctor?"

"I'm old, but I'm not that old that I need to be fussed over for a little tumble. Help me up." She dusted off, muttering and shaking her head. "Booby-traps, I told you. You wouldn't believe me."

Drake toed the rope with his boot. Nothing happened. "I think this is a case of messiness more than nefariousness." He winked, bending to pick up the rope, but as he pulled, a scraping sounded.

Evie hightailed it out of the room, screaming, as fast as her short legs would carry her.

Raegan, stifling a laugh, watched as the rope came out from the table, the other end tied around a small black box with rounded corners. Drake lifted it up for her inspection, and upon a closer look, she saw that it wasn't truly black but rather a very deep brown. By all appearances, the box was made from a portion of hollowed-out old tree trunk. Carved into the center of the lid was a pot of gold. When Raegan pressed the pot of gold, the lid sprung open, revealing a velvet pouch of dark emerald green.

"Is this your dad's, too?" Drake asked.

Raegan shrugged. "It must be, but I've never seen it before. I've never seen any of this before."

Evie poked her head around the doorway. "Is it safe?"

Drake motioned her in. "Come see. Raegan was about to open up another hidden treasure."

That piqued Evie's interest enough that she hurried back to their sides. Raegan placed the box on the table and pulled out the velvet pouch. Slowly, she pulled the drawstring opening wider and slipped her hand inside.

Beside her, Evie's breath caught. "Well? What is it?"

Raegan saw Drake struggle to contain a laugh at the excitable older woman.

She pulled the contents from the bag and spread them on the table. Raegan picked up a worn compass tied on a leather chord like a necklace. Engraved on the back was part of an Irish blessing addressed to her.

Rae, may the road rise up to meet you, the wind be always at your back, and may the sun shine warm upon your face, my lovely.

"Beautiful." Evie swiped at a stray tear.

Raegan slipped the leather chord over her head, tucking the compass near her heart, before lifting the next item. It was a beautiful shamrock hair comb inlaid with four small emeralds that sparkled brilliantly as they caught the light. As she turned it over, one of the two prongs separated from the comb, and she saw that it was a miniature dagger.

Evie fluttered a hand over her heart, eyes wide, while Drake gave a low whistle. "Remind me to never underestimate the power of women dressing up again."

"There's just one more thing." Raegan unfolded the last item from the pouch, a worn and creased sheaf of papers. She scanned the first page. "Hold on. This can't be right."

"What is it?" Drake asked.

Evie shuffled from one foot to the other. "Is it a treasure map? Are there more secret rooms?" Having recovered from her fright, she was returning to her usual fanciful self.

"It's a deed."

"To the library?" Drake asked.

Raegan dragged her gaze from the papers. "No. To a castle. In Ireland."

Her announcement was met with shocked silence.

"It can't be right, though. I mean, I can't own a castle in Ireland. How ridiculous does that sound?" Raegan flipped through the sheaf of papers as if looking for a big sign to spring forth and say *gotcha*.

"Oh! My goodness! You have a secret room and a secret castle? I've got to sit down." Evie sagged onto an armchair in the corner.

Drake stayed quiet until finally Raegan couldn't stand it anymore. "Well, you've nothing to say? Did you know about all of this?"

"Not a thing," Drake denied. "I only know what I told you upstairs."

Raegan frowned, studying him. If only she knew how to tell if he were lying or not. Unfortunately, her radar for that sort of thing was nonexistent. She simply didn't interact with people enough. Should she trust him?

Drake, seeming to sense her hesitation, rubbed the back of his neck. "The only other thing is, well," he glanced at Evie and lowered his voice, "I thought it was odd, but the League did refer to you as a princess quite a lot."

"No."

"What?"

"No." Raegan tossed the papers down. "No. I am not a princess. This is not funny. I don't know what is going on, but I have got to get out of here." With that, she jabbed the shamrock comb into her bun and strode out of the room.

*　　　　*　　　　*

Minutes after hearing the bang of the large library doors shutting, Drake knelt and picked up the papers that Raegan had discarded.

Snoring from the corner told him that Evie had fallen asleep. No doubt she had experienced more excitement that day than perhaps the rest of the century. Drake tucked the velvet pouch back into its box and placed them on the desk. He carried the papers with him to one of the many reading areas in the main library, far enough away where he could look over them without disturbing Evie but close enough to hear if she became startled again and called out.

Raegan would be back sometime. He would wait for her. Maybe by then, he would be able to help her make sense of her new property. He couldn't help but be a little thrilled. If she owned a castle in Ireland, she would want to see it. Who wouldn't? Maybe, just maybe, it was what he finally needed to get her to travel back with him.

12.

C ome on," Raegan implored. "You can't be serious. You don't think me owning a castle in Ireland is a little far-fetched? Or this…this…League of Leprechauns, whoever they are, being interested in me is crazy?" She sat in the kitchen of Lorcan's pub, pouring out the whole story between bites of shepherd's pie. Stress eating had seemed the best course of action, especially since her growling stomach reminded her that she'd skipped lunch.

"A bit sudden, maybe. Something of a surprise, sure. But I must tell you, lass, I had my suspicions that your da' was one of the wee folks, I did I tell you." Lorcan shook a big meaty finger at her. "And not just because he was short. No, had a funny way of talking, he did. Loved a good joke. And always a blessing on his lips. Never a bad thing to say. He had this way about him." Lorcan stood a moment, smiling into the distance, clearly remembering.

Raegan couldn't take it. "You think my father was a leprechaun," she spluttered. "But aren't leprechauns supposed to hoard gold? And make shoes? My dad owned a library! He never cobbled a shoe in the twelve years I knew him."

"Now, now. Nothing to be upset over." Lorcan patted her shoulder. "Whether he was or he weren't doesn't matter much. The fact of the matter is that your da' made sure you were heir to your ma's castle. That means he trusted you to take care of it. So, what are you going to do?"

Raegan pushed mashed potatoes around grumpily with her fork. "Trusted me to take care of it but didn't think it important enough to mention. Hmph!" She took a bite.

"Maybe he planned to tell you when you were older," Joan spoke softly. She had remained quiet for most of the discussion. "Maybe he simply ran out of time."

Tears burned the back of Raegan's eyes. She wished her dad was there. She wanted to ask him about his past, about the castle, about all of it.

"Maybe you're right." Raegan carried her empty plate to the sink. She gave them both a hug. "I promise to think about it and to let you know if I decide to go see the castle or to meet with the League."

"We are here for you." Joan hugged her back.

Lorcan grinned. "You'll do the right thing. You're like your da' in that."

13.

What do you mean you've never been on a boat before?" Drake watched as Raegan fidgeted with the picnic basket from Lorcan in her hands and stared warily at the ferry as they made their way toward it.

"There wasn't any reason to." Raegan shrugged. "Besides, in books, many people love boats but just as many people get seasick, or even shipwrecked."

Drake shook his head. "There is more to life than books, you know."

"There is also more life *in books* than most people will ever know in their single lifetime," Raegan countered.

When their turn came, Drake saw Raegan hesitate. He held out his hand, and warmth stirred through him as she took it. They stepped on together, him tugging her forward around the milling people.

"Where are we going?"

"You'll see." The ferry began moving, and Raegan clutched his hand tighter. Drake continued to lead her to the front of the small boat. "Here we are," he said, coming to a stop at the railing. In front of them lay only water.

Raegan set the picnic basket by her feet, carefully placing her backpack on top, and dropped his hand to clutch the rail. "Is this safe? Shouldn't we go find somewhere to sit down?"

Drake chuckled. "Relax. Just look."

*   *   *

Raegan took a deep breath. As she looked out over the expanse of sea, the most magical thing happened. "Are those dolphins?" she gasped. She watched as the two beautiful creatures jumped and squeaked, seeming to beg the ferry to come and play. She laughed at their antics, her fingers uncurling from the rail.

From the corner of her eye, she noticed her backpack moving around. She retrieved it, sticking a few fingers into the largest pocket. Unfortunately, that was not enough comfort for Nessa, and she let out a loud meow. As Drake turned in surprise, Raegan felt her cheeks heat up.

"I had to bring her!" she defended before he could say a word. "It isn't fair to leave the library up to Evie, even with Joan volunteering to help out, and also expect them to care for Nessa."

Drake rolled his eyes.

Eventually, the dolphins ceased their antics and disappeared from sight. The rest of the ferry ride passed pleasantly if uneventfully. She and Drake did find a bench outside so she could continue to enjoy the sights, and as they made their journey to Ireland, they discussed the papers again.

"It's so hard to believe that Dún Castle was in my mother's family for generations." With the deed, her dad had enclosed a long letter explaining that her mother had been cut off from her family for marrying him. However, with no other heirs, the family home and surrounding land had remained her mother's, even in her absence. Before she died, her mother willed everything to Raegan. It seemed Raegan's dad had made certain to see to it that everything transferred properly. The only thing that was left was for Raegan to actually claim the castle—she couldn't think of it as her home yet—and file the papers with the proper authorities in County Galway.

What would it be like to walk into the home where her mother had lived? Would she feel the connection, the presence of her mother, that she'd never had before? Would it be warm and welcoming? Or terrible and cold, invoking thoughts of her mother being shunned and disowned by her family? The letter from her father explained that her grandfather had never willed the castle to another person as he'd threatened, but let it pass to her mother instead. Why hadn't he ever made peace with her mother, then? Sighing for the umpteenth time, Raegan tried to shove aside all of her doubts and anxieties.

She decided to focus on the practical, the next steps.

Raegan stroked Nessa, the kitten purring contentedly in her lap. "Where will we go when we arrive in Ireland?"

"We'll take a bus from Dublin to Galway. From there, a smaller bus line will take us the rest of the way to Glas, the town where my pub is at. I need to check in, and you can rest a bit before we make the last short leg of the journey by foot to Kilvarleigh, the village where Dún Castle is located." Drake stretched. "The ferry is the longest part of the journey. Speaking of long, it is long past time to bring out whatever smells so heavenly from the basket, wouldn't you say?"

Handing Nessa to Drake, Raegan obliged. She opened the basket and rummaged around, naming off foods as she unpacked them. "Here we are. Grilled chicken. Soda bread. Hummus. Carrot sticks. And two miniature apple tarts." Spread out between them on the bench, the food looked like a veritable feast, and Raegan felt the first stab of homesickness slice through her. Lorcan, for all his blessings and well wishes, had shed a few tears of his own that morning as she bid him and Joan farewell at the library. They'd insisted on bringing over food for the ferry ride, even though that meant seeing them off from the library before daybreak. She'd laughed, telling them she would return in no time, but in truth she didn't know how long dealing with the castle, plus possibly meeting the surreptitious League of Leprechauns, might take. She missed her surrogate family dearly already.

"What is this fuzzball going to eat?" Drake asked, snapping her free of her thoughts as he thrust Nessa back at her. A cat person he evidently was not.

"I'll share my chicken with her. If I make it small enough, I'm sure she'll do fine." They ate in silence, the only sound that of the water lapping against the sides of the ferry and the gulls crying overhead. Nessa enjoyed the chicken, perhaps a little too much. Raegan struggled to keep the kitten from swatting her own bites from her hand. Finally, she took the ribbon out of her hair and made a makeshift leash, tying Nessa to one leg of the bench and placing plenty of tiny bites within her reach.

"So, why were you so eager to swoop into a different country and convince a stranger to go to Ireland?" She asked one of the many questions that had cropped up since she learned the real reason that he'd come to the library what felt like ages before.

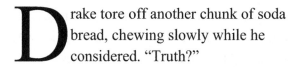

14.

Drake tore off another chunk of soda bread, chewing slowly while he considered. "Truth?"

"That would be my preference from now on," Raegan said wryly.

Drake nodded. "Because I was well on my way to becoming a drunk, swaying somewhere between depressed and mad at the world. And I was broke. My father was a gambling man, only he never met a bet he could win. When he died, he left me the pub because he'd already lost the house. Truth be told, the pub was about to go under, too. I was angry at him for leaving such a mess of things and angry at myself for missing him so much while I was mad at him."

Raegan simply listened, so he continued.

"The night the four men from the League came in, I was in bad shape. I quit my job days earlier, in no shape to help others when I couldn't help myself. I'd just had a barstool busted over my head hours before by an idiot starting fights in the pub. I'd drank a whole bottle of Irish whiskey, and I was tired. Tired of the way my life was going." Drake shrugged. "When they showed up with their fantastic tale and their odd quirks and tricks, I was curious and amused. And I couldn't remember the last time that I'd felt either of those things."

Raegan nodded. "I understand."

"The bag of gold they pushed under my nose next, well, that is a horse of a different color." Drake leaned back and stretched out his legs, folding his arms behind his head. "It was enough to save the pub, pay back most of the debts, and even make some improvements. We were in need of new barstools, if you'll recall."

Raegan laughed, and Drake suddenly wanted nothing more than to make her laugh again. The thought took him by surprise. To cover his discomfort, he straightened and pulled off another chunk of bread to eat. "Tell me more about you. It must have been interesting growing up with Lorcan and Joan."

"Interesting is a good word for it, though I was almost a teen by the time I began living with them. I knew them, of course. A fast friend of my dad's, Lorcan was always around. He met Joan when I was little. I can't remember exactly when." Raegan considered. "Joan was as quiet as Lorcan was loud, but she was always there with a kind word, a bandage, or a warm hug. When I started doing badly in school after my dad passed, she simply took up teaching me at home, and I never went back."

"She's English, not Irish, am I correct?"

"Yes, that's right." Raegan smiled. "She tried to introduce me to some nice young men for a time, but most of them were appalled to find that I spent all of my time with my nose in a book."

Drake's chest constricted at the thought of Raegan dating, or even being snubbed and overlooked when dating. He decided to change the subject again. "What do you like to read?"

"Everything. My favorites would be adventure stories or love conquers all stories. My parents were truly in love. You could still see it in my father's eyes when he talked about my mother twelve years after she'd been gone. Evidently, they gave up everything for each other—their lives, their families, their country." Raegan sighed. "Love isn't worth having if it isn't worth everything, you know?"

Nessa, out of chicken and out of patience, meowed and clawed at Raegan's shoe. *Saved by the cat,* Drake thought. He bent and put a bit more chicken on the ground for the feisty feline and then started packing up their leftovers.

The remaining few hours of the ferry trip, Raegan and Drake stuck to lighter topics. As the afternoon sun burned hot overhead, Raegan drifted off to sleep.

*　　　　　*　　　　　*

Raegan blinked slowly as she tried to remember where she was. She felt warm and snug, but it was so bright. There was no way she was home in her bed. Something shifted behind her.

Definitely not her bed. Her bed did not shift.

Raegan bolted upright as she realized she'd fallen asleep leaning against Drake. She straightened her rumpled appearance and patted her hair but forgot all about how she looked when she faced Drake. Her heart melted just a little to see sweet Nessa curled up around his neck, fast asleep. The smallest smile tugged at her lips. She and Nessa would turn him into a cat person yet.

Two short blasts of the ferry horn signaled they were approaching port. Unfortunately, they also signaled the end of

Nessa's peaceful nap. The kitten sank its claws into Drake's shoulder and hissed madly before leaping down his arm and onto Raegan's lap.

"I'm so sorry!" Raegan apologized.

Drake brushed off her concern. "It's fine. Let's get to the front of the line to disembark." He picked up the picnic basket and swung her backpack over his shoulder with his own.

Raegan followed him, quietly chastising Nessa along the way.

15.

At the port, Drake led Raegan to a bus stop where they took a complimentary connecting line to the main bus station. The hustle and bustle of the station took Raegan by surprise. Not to mention, it was so much busier than anywhere she'd ever been. She found herself people-watching instead of paying attention and twice nearly tripped over her own feet. Nessa didn't help matters at all, alternately digging her claws into Raegan's shirt or trying to jump down to investigate something.

"Are you coming?"

Raegan detached Nessa's tiny, sharp claws from her arm and nodded. "Yes. Right behind you." She hurried to get in line with

Drake as he bought them tickets to Galway Station. "How long is our bus ride?"

"A little over two hours." Drake set the bags and picnic basket down in front of the ticket window so he could reach his wallet. "Nothing compared to spending all day on the ferry."

"Oh, okay." Raegan scanned the station. Everything was a novelty. The noise of buses pulling in or out every few minutes, people yelling, the smells of smoke and perfumes. Her senses were going crazy.

"Raegan. Rae!"

Jolted, Raegan looked up to find that Drake was across the room and holding the door open to her expectantly. Raegan, tightening her grip on Nessa, skirted in and out of people and joined him outside.

"Well?"

"Well, what?" Raegan asked.

Drake gestured to the buses, the people, the luggage stacked everywhere they looked. "What do you think?"

"It's so much busier than I expected," Raegan admitted. She spun in a slow circle, taking it all in. A bus honked nearby, making her jump. A toddler began screaming and crying as his mother carried him toward the bus. "And louder," she frowned.

"Don't worry," Drake said. "The village where we're going is quiet. Almost completely quiet, unless you count the occasional bleat of a sheep or squabbling of some well-meaning farmers about the best direction to lay out the rows of crops in the fields."

Across the street from the bus station was a pub and next door to that a haberdashery. Down the row of buildings, a hat store stood out, along with a flower shop. Of course, such shops were common in England as well. Raegan shouldn't have been so excited about it all, but she was. It was her very own adventure, and nervous as she might be, she determined to enjoy every bit of it.

There were similarities to home, as well, mostly in the faces of passersby. Everyone looked busy. Few stopped to greet one another, instead bustling along to their destination in quick, efficient strides. In no time at all, Drake tapped her on the shoulder and said that their bus had arrived.

Drake stowed their belongings below the seats and was dozing against the window before the bus even left the station. Raegan watched him guiltily. Maybe if she hadn't slept and left him to deal with Nessa on the ferry, he would have caught some rest earlier. With Drake asleep and blocking most of the window, she ran out of distractions, and her thoughts quickly grew nervous again. *What would she find in Kivarleigh? What was she supposed to do with a castle? And how in the world did the League think she was going to save the village?* According to Drake, they hadn't even said what it needed saving from.

Unable to still her restless thoughts, Raegan turned to the one thing that always calmed her mind: reading. Careful not to let go of Nessa with one hand, she rustled around beneath the seats until she came up with her backpack. From it, she pulled out one of many books she had brought about Ireland. That one happened to be about Irish fairy tales and legends. She lost herself in whimsical descriptions of fairies and sprites and shuddered at the thought of meeting an Abhartach, or Irish vampire.

By the time they reached Galway, she had completely read through the legends, delving into the next book detailing the history of Ireland. A bit drier reading, to be sure, but at least it didn't contain the stuff that nightmares were made of.

The loud brake and shuddering stop of the bus roused Drake from his long nap.

Rae smiled over at him. "We've made it to Galway, I guess."

As they stepped off the bus, Drake glanced around. "Aye. Let's catch our next ride then."

"Let me guess," Raegan pointed. "Another bus?"

"Yes, but then that is it. We'll be there in no time and able to stretch our legs on the walk from the pub to the village where your, erm, holdings are supposed to be."

Raegan appreciated Drake not pointing out again that she owned a castle. It was still too far-fetched for her to think about. She was simply going to take it one step at a time.

The bus ride to Kivarleigh proved pleasant enough. Seated by the window, Raegan enjoyed watching the scenery change from the bustling harborside city bursting at the seams with people, to smaller less populated towns, to quaint rural villages. Nessa swatted at the glass for a time, eventually wearing herself out and settling down to a nap as well. When at last their stop arrived, it was in such a place. The noise and bustle of the better part of the day were gone. A quietness met them. A woman arranging flowers in a window box smiled and waved. A girl on a bicycle beeped her small horn at them. Raegan smiled at the loveliness of it all.

"The pub is just around the corner," Drake motioned. "I'll have a check inside, set the bags down, and we can be on our way."

Raegan followed, matching his quick strides, determined not to fall behind again. The Keeper's Keg wasn't what she expected. The nameplate hung askew. The door hinges needed oiling, judging by the squeak loud enough to rouse the dead. And the inside was drabber than drab. The pub literally had no personality. Perhaps she judged it too harshly, familiar as she was with The Red Deer and Lorcan's larger than life presence back home. Still, she found she wasn't surprised that Drake had been struggling with depression, losing his father and living there alone as he had been.

Raegan let Nessa down to explore as she continued to wander around the small space. Drake spoke to the man behind the bar—she'd already forgotten his name—and then stowed their bags upstairs until they saw the condition of Raegan's home. Home didn't fit any better than castle when she said it in her mind, but she found herself hoping that would change when she saw it.

"Ready for that walk?" Drake asked, joining her by the door.

"Definitely," Raegan answered honestly. She adjusted the strap of a small purse she'd brought over her shoulder. It had all of the documents concerning the estate. Her mother's estate. Though the papers had been left to her by her father, they clearly stated the castle and lands were coming to her through her mother's line. Evidently, there had been no male heirs. It was bittersweet knowing she would be seeing where her mother had lived but also the place where family had turned their back on her. Would her mother have ever come back? Would she be glad that Raegan was going? Or would she have told her to stay away? Her thoughts swirled around and around as she mused.

Drake paused. "Wait just a second." He stooped behind the bar and came back with a smaller picnic basket that he'd stuffed a soft towel inside. "For Nessa." He handed her the basket.

Raegan smiled. "Thank you! My arms were getting a little tired of being used as pincushions." She settled Nessa inside the basket, poured a capful of water for her to drink, and after several refills for the thirsty kitten, they headed back outside. Nessa curled up sleepily, content to ride along, thank goodness.

They walked in silence for ten minutes or more. The village disappeared behind them quickly, giving way to land as far as the eye could see, rugged and beautiful. At last, Raegan couldn't take it anymore.

"It's so incredible," she burst out. "I never minded living in the city, really didn't notice if I'm being honest. But here, the hills. The green! The flowers!" At that moment they rounded a bend and came upon a flock of sheep grazing, a few moseying along across the road, and Raegan laughed out loud. "The animals who are in no hurry." She tucked a strand of unruly hair back into her ponytail as she shook her head. "Everyone hurries in the city. Very few people even came to the library that weren't rushing in and out. The library for goodness sakes! That should be a place to slow down, relax, and browse the worlds awaiting you inside the pages."

Becoming self-conscious of Drake watching her, Raegan ducked her head. "Sorry. I get a little carried away."

*   *   *

Drake found himself entranced as Raegan spread her arms and spun, gushing about the landscape of his country. Then, she launched into the cutest little tirade about her beloved library, and he nearly laughed out loud. As Raegan turned and caught his gaze on her, heat creeping into her cheeks, Drake couldn't help but murmur, "Beautiful."

At Raegan's quizzical frown, he cleared his throat. "Beautiful country, you're right," he amended. "Come. We aren't far now."

Drake took the lead back and headed down the road, left at a fork where the road narrowed to more of a single and poorly paved lane. The paving soon gave way to dirt. Drake paused to let Raegan catch up as he crested the last hill. Raegan's gasp of awe was all that he expected as she laid eyes on the land below. He watched as her eyes widened, her hands covering her mouth as her jaw dropped. Her skin fairly glowed with excitement. It was contagious. Drake reached for her hand as it dropped to her side.

"M'lady." He waved his other arm with a flourish, bowing low. "Your castle awaits."

16.

Raegan's breath caught in her throat as she surveyed the rolling hillside below them. Even Drake's silly comment about her castle waiting couldn't spoil the moment. It was like nothing she'd ever seen before.

Rolling fields laid out like an emerald-green patchwork quilt with low stone walls providing borders between all shapes and sizes of gorgeous blocks of land. Eight or ten cottages dotted the hillside, with another bunch huddled together along the bottom of the slope where the bright green grass met dark gray and black stones tumbling into the cliffside.

And there, just as Drake said, at the furthest point down the shore, sprawled more stone walls surrounding a tall, gray stone castle, not much longer than it was wide, with a taller wall enclosing a courtyard.

Her mother's family home.

The thought squeezed at her heart.

The castle itself was mere feet above the shoreline, built at the only area where tall cliffs didn't make such a location impossible.

Slowly, Raegan realized that she had been staring for quite some time. She also became acutely aware that Drake had been holding her hand as she did. Ignoring the warm tingles dancing inside her, she withdrew the hand under the pretense of tucking another piece of hair behind her ear. The breeze liberated it again immediately.

She licked her lips and smiled. "I can taste the sea."

Drake nodded. "You'll be feeling the sand between your toes in no time. Are you ready to see it?"

She knew he referred to the castle, not the sea. Inhaling another breath of salty air, she gave a firm nod. "Let's go."

The walk down the hillside was easy and pleasurable. They passed a few more sheep and some sheep dogs. At one of the cottages close to the road, a woman out hanging laundry on a line hailed them.

"Haven't seen the likes of you two here before." She smiled as Nessa poked her head out of the basket. "Pardon me, you three, I mean. I'm Shauna. Are you visiting?"

"Sort of," Raegan shrugged. "We're going to see Dún Castle. I'm not sure yet if we'll be staying in the area." She introduced herself and Drake. "And this little ball of fur is Nessa."

"Dún Castle, ay? There've been a lot of visitors to the old place lately." Shauna frowned. "Are you tourists?"

"No, not tourists, though I'd happily take the chance be one in this beautiful country. Actually, we're here because the castle belongs to my mother's family. To me." Raegan answered truthfully. Interested, she couldn't help but ask, "Were there other tourists here? The visitors you mentioned."

"No. Lord Donovan."

"I've heard that name before," Drake said. "Typically, at the end of a curse in my pub over in the next village."

Shauna nodded, face grim. "He's not well-liked and for good reason. Fancies himself better than us regular folk, but he bought himself that fancy title. His blood is no more special than my pig out back. Donovan owns most of this land, mine included. Charges rents most can ill-afford. Why half the cottages are empty, the villagers simply giving up and leaving." Her hands balled up the towel in her hand, her words clipped. "He's driving them out on purpose. Wants to build some fancy resort here, and if we're gone, the way is wide open, and the profits are all his."

"That's terrible!" Raegan said.

"He probably would have succeeded long ago if it weren't for one thing."

"What's that?" Drake asked.

"Dún Castle. He could never find a way to get his hands on it legally." Shauna patted Raegan on the shoulder. "But mark my words, he's still looking for something down there. And he's one to keep your eye on very closely."

Drake and Raegan thanked her for the chat and continued on their way.

"It's a good thing we're almost there." Raegan stroked Nessa's soft fur. "Someone is getting a little restless."

"She should have plenty of nooks and crannies to explore shortly," Drake said.

Using Nessa as her excuse, Raegan picked up her pace. They weren't far from the outer wall of the castle, and if she were being honest, excitement hummed through her.

A castle.

A real-life castle!

She couldn't help it. Every fairy tale, enchanted kingdom adventure, or historical fiction novel that she had ever read raced through her brain. She was geeking-out on the inside.

Between the scenes flitting through her imagination and the fact that she couldn't take her eyes off the ancient structure looming in front of them, she didn't see the rock.

It was a small rock, mixed among plenty of other rocks, not dissimilar to the same rocks in the path they'd been treading for miles and miles. Unfortunately, that rock was covered with just enough moss to cause her foot to slip. Raegan cried out as she felt her ankle twist.

As she stumbled, the basket lurched sideways, and Nessa flew out, rolling safely in the grass by the road. The curious kitten batted the green blades around before loping down the hill and through the arched entrance of the castle courtyard.

"Nessa!" Raegan called out. She moved to chase after the wayward kitten but grimaced as pain sliced through her ankle.

Drake reached out and caught her arm. "Let me take a look at that foot."

"But Nessa."

"Look," Drake pointed calmly. "She's inside the courtyard, exactly where we're going. You'll find her in no time. Maybe she'll rid the place of mice while she waits for us."

Raegan continued to grumble but stood still as Drake felt around her ankle. She gritted her teeth as he mashed and squeezed.

"Put pressure on it," he said.

She did and regretted it. "Ow!" she yelped. Trying again, she put pressure only on her toes and managed to hobble two steps before sinking to the ground. "Maybe we should just rest. I'm sure it'll be fine in a few minutes."

Drake rolled his eyes at her. "Can you hold on to your bag and the basket?" he asked.

"Yes…" Raegan thought it a strange question. She'd been carrying it that far, after all. Why should sitting them in the grass for a moment make any difference?

Before she could ask, Drake plopped both in her lap and slipped his arms beneath her legs and armpits, scooping her effortlessly from the ground.

"Excuse me," Raegan spluttered. "This is ridiculous. I can walk."

"Except you can't. You tried." Drake said pointedly, raising an eyebrow.

Raegan glared. "Put me down. I'll try again."

"I thought you wanted to find Nessa."

Raegan narrowed her eyes and wished for the power to shoot laser beams from them like Superman. She would roast that smirk right from Drake's mouth. His gloating expression had her plotting payback at the first possible turn. Maybe she'd fire him from the library.

Of course, she worried, *he might not want to return anyway*. Maybe she could sic Nessa on him in his sleep. She grinned, thinking about his discomfort with the tiny animal.

"Whatever you're thinking, it can't be good."

Raegan's grin broadened. "I've no idea what you're talking about."

Once through the wall to the courtyard, Raegan was too distracted to stay mad. She worked to close her mouth, certain she'd felt her jaw drop as she stared up at the moss-covered stone tower-house before them. Smaller than many of the castles and manors she had glimpsed along their route, the structure stood imposing nonetheless. The battlements were missing a stone here and there, but overall, the fortress looked quite formidable. The wall they had entered through to the courtyard, or bailey, was a good three feet thick. She knew from reading that many castle walls were up to seven feet thick. Between the relative thinness of the walls and the fact that the keep was not built at a higher elevation, Raegan assumed that her mother's home must not have fallen under attack too often when it was built.

Drawing her eyes back down to the grounds where they stood and the surrounding area, Raegan pointed to the small door in the gatehouse next to them which stood ajar. "Let's check for Nessa in there, please."

It took a few moments for her eyes to adjust to the darkness inside the small building. The room they entered appeared to be a kitchen and mudroom. A modern stove and refrigerator took her by surprise. They passed through it quickly.

Drake sat her carefully on a couch in the second room, which turned out to be a bit larger and much brighter than the kitchen, thanks to a beautiful four-paned window on one side of the room.

Raegan was equally astonished to see that the main living area was also furnished and clean. For some reason, she'd been expecting everything to be abandoned and empty. Could it be that someone still lived there? A relative of her mother's? Squatters?

Her bouncing thoughts were interrupted by Drake. "I'll search while you sit tight a minute." He called for Nessa, looking beneath furniture and behind the curtains. He stepped through another door, which turned out to be a tiny bathroom. With no sign of Nessa there either, he gave the kitchen a thorough going over and returned in minutes, shrugging. "Sorry. No luck. I'm sure she's just exploring further in."

Raegan frowned.

*   *   *

Drake delivered the news to Raegan. As he watched her disappointment at hearing there was no sign of Nessa wash all excitement from her face, it made him wish he'd found the blasted cat after all. Apart from her sadness, he could also see her gearing up for an argument about searching the rest of the castle It was in the telltale way her mouth tightened and her eyes narrowed, creating that deep *v* between her finely arched eyebrows.

Crossing his arms, he spoke first, hoping to put a stop to her plan before she could voice it. "I'll go out and search the whole grounds for that little furball if, and only if, you promise to stay here and remain off of that ankle."

Raegan's lips pursed into a tiny pout. She seemed to consider her options. Worry for Nessa clearly won out over her irritation at being bossed around. It was all Drake could do not to laugh as she blew out a resigned breath and agreed in a sullen grumble.

True to his word, Drake began a methodical search. He swept the courtyard first, checking behind the gatehouse as well as keeping an eye out for any holes or gaps in the wall where the kitten might have wandered back out into the countryside. Turning up nothing in front, Drake made his way around the side of the castle.

He hoped for Raegan's sake that the wall continued all the way around. If the kitten had made it out to the ocean, well, he'd rather not think about the possibilities.

17.

Raegan scooted back on the couch. She leaned to the left, tried propping her elbow up on the throw pillows, tucked her good foot beneath her, then stretched it out again. She sighed, throwing her head back on the couch. It was useless. She couldn't get comfortable.

"Drat this stupid ankle," she growled to the empty room. She was itching to get outside and help Drake look for Nessa, dying not to feel completely helpless. It would be so awful if she'd saved the sweet, albeit feisty kitten from the dingy alley only to lose her in Ireland. Maybe she should have left her behind after all.

"Time to think about something else," she told herself. Digging around in her purse, she pulled out a new book with a triumphant smile. The book featured the flora and fauna of Ireland. With a mind to try a reverse scavenger hunt, Raegan thumbed through the pages in search of flowers, birds, and even grasses that they had passed on their journey there.

Half an hour later, lost in the pages brimming with beautiful photographs, Raegan didn't hear the front door open and close, nor did she catch the sound of footsteps drawing closer. A sharp clearing of a throat startled her. The book flew from her hands, landing on the floor with a thump. She cringed, hoping it hadn't been damaged.

"Hello," she said to the stranger standing across the small room. "Do you live here? I'm sorry for intruding. I twisted my ankle and needed a place to rest."

His steely gaze and upturned nose made her comfortable. The suit he wore looked like it must have cost a fortune, all perfectly fitted tight lines, gold cuff links, and polished shoes. Nothing about him fit her romanticized idea of an Irishman.

"Who are you?" the stranger asked, flaring his nostrils, mouth crinkling in disgust as he inspected Raegan from head to toe.

Raegan ignored the feeling of being found wanting and pulled her shoulders back before introducing herself. "I'm Raegan Sheridan, the heir of Dún Castle."

"Heir, ay?" The stranger's unkind face crinkled into a beaming smiled. "Welcome to Ireland, Miss Sheridan. I am Lord Donovan. You could say we're neighbors, as I own most of the land visible from your little castle. I must say, I'm surprised to find you here. I was unaware old Sheridan had any other heirs after he disowned his only daughter. Tragic, all that. You look very much like her."

Raegan gawked. The way he said that last bit, it didn't sound at all like a compliment.

Charm oozed from Lord Donovan like honey oozed from a bottle, thick and sticky, covering everything. If she hadn't witnessed the transformation on his face from harsh to polite, she would have thought he was just the kindest soul ever. As it was, he gave her the creeps.

"It is lovely to meet you," she managed to say. She refused to address his comments about her grandfather, her mother, or her being the heir.

"Well, no matter where you came from, I'm glad you're here."

"Oh?" Raegan's mouth formed around the word slowly. It was the last thing she'd expected him to say.

"Yes. I've been attempting to buy the castle for several years now, but I kept hitting red tape. I'll give you two hundred and ten thousand euro. Today." Lord Donovan extracted a checkbook from his breast pocket. "I'll even escort you back to the train or bus, whichever you prefer, as I didn't see any particular conveyance outside."

Raegan stared, her brain working overtime to process the outrageous man's proposal. The villager, Shauna, had mentioned Lord Donovan's interest in the property, but she hadn't expected him to approach her to buy it.

"Would you spell your first name for me?" Lord Donovan had a pen poised over the checkbook.

The high-handed offer and outrageous assumption that she would sell to him on less than one conversation irked her. Raegan shifted forward and stood, placing weight on her good leg only. Her scowl covered her wince, at least she hoped it did.

"I'm afraid I'm not looking to sell at the moment. I've only just arrived, and I'd like to see the place and consider my options before I make a decision as to whether or not I'll be staying."

Staying. Raegan surprised herself with the comment but found in her heart she was already considering it, though the castle interior remained unseen. There was something wild and whimsical about the country that was already taking root in her soul. A soft smile settled on her face as she daydreamed about the possibilities.

Unfortunately, she was the only one smiling.

"Options?" Lord Donovan's smile vanished, wiped away as if by an eraser. He lowered his voice, nostrils flaring once more. "Let me make your options abundantly clear. You can stay and be driven from this ancient pile of stone the hard way, or you can leave with a nice fat check and memories of a lovely holiday to the Irish coast to share with people wherever it is that you came from." Lord Donovan menaced forward with each word.

Raegan shrank backward, bumping into the couch and falling onto it.

Lord Donovan took advantage of her vulnerability, swooping closer. He leaned toward her, white knuckles gripping the checkbook as he waved it at her. "You have three days to make your decision. Each day you delay, I drop twenty thousand euros from my more than generous offer."

Raegan couldn't have answered if she wanted to. Words, normally some of her favorite companions, had abandoned her. She sat stock still, rooted in shock even after Lord Donovan stomped out of the room, the front door slamming shut in his wake.

Not fifteen seconds later, she heard the door open again. Certain the odious man had returned, Raegan scrambled to her feet. She gritted her teeth, standing tall and firm. Footsteps shuffled toward her, and the murmur of a voice—maybe more than one—made their way to her. She glanced around, wondering if Lord Donovan had gone outside for reinforcements. Throw pillows and a blanket, hand-crocheted by all appearances, were the only items near her. She thought quickly, reaching into her hair and pulling out the shamrock hair comb, the dagger from her father. Wielding it in front of her, she waited.

"Whoa, there, lass!" A tall, lanky gentlemen at least seventy or better raised his hands in surprise as he stepped into the living area. His brogue was considerably thicker than any she'd heard to that point, even Lorcan's, and that was saying something.

Raegan frowned. The man didn't look like much of a threat. And by his woolen clothes and muddy shoes, she wouldn't have taken him for an associate of the slicked-back Lord Donovan either.

Meow.

Drake rounded the doorframe, and a small ball of fur catapulted from his arms.

"Nessa," Raegan exhaled in relief, slipping the comb back into her hair. She lowered herself to the couch and caught the kitten as it climbed awkwardly up her legs and into her lap, cradling it to her chest. "Thank you for finding her."

Nessa's purring was audible; clearly the kitten was grateful to have been found as well. Raegan snuggled her closer.

"It wasn't me," Drake said. "This is Conor. He and Nessa were getting acquainted when I found them. Conor, meet

Raegan Sheridan. She's the one I was telling you about."

"A pleasure, it is, lass. Conor O'Malley, at your service." He pointed a finger at Nessa. "That girl there found me while I was cleaning inside the castle. Must have snuck in to look for mice, but she'll be mighty disappointed. I don't tolerate mice." Conor extended a hand to shake. "I hope you don't mind that I've stayed on in the gatehouse. I'm the groundskeeper and keeper of, well, generally everything here since I'm the only one left. Knew your ma, I did. Been lookin' after the place, hoping someday she'd find her way back here." He tipped his head. "Sorry for your loss."

Raegan's eyes misted. "You knew her?"

"Aye, since she was a wee lass." Conor smiled broadly. "She had her fair share of twisted ankles, too, I remember." He winked. "If ye think ye can get this strapping young man here to carry you inside, I know where there's a wheelchair left you can use, and I'll show ye all of your ma's portraits in the gallery."

Drake did not wait for permission, reaching her in two strides and picking Raegan, and Nessa, up from the couch.

"Did my old eyes deceive me, or did I see Lord Donovan going out of the gate when we came in, lass?" Conor asked as they crossed the courtyard to the large wooden door on the castle.

Raegan reflexively tightened her arm around Drake's neck. "Yes. He dropped by to make sure I knew I would be unwelcomed here." Her mouth tightened. "Apparently, the man is as dastardly as the rumors we heard." With a little prompting, she filled the men in on the confrontation in Conor's living room.

"Donovan's never been good at hearing the word no. Thinks he can do whatever he bloody wants, and for the most part, he's been right." Conor's face darkened. "Been a few times I woke to find fire outside the gatehouse and inside the castle. Can't prove it, mind, but I'd bet me best shovel it was Donovan, the snake."

"Why does he want Dún Castle so badly?" Raegan asked, settling into the wheelchair Conor had rolled out of a hall closet. "Does he hope to rent out the property like so many others I'm told he owns in this area?"

"If only that were the case, lass." Conor said woefully. "Lord Donovan is a greedy man. He thought your grandfather would leave the castle to him once your mother left. Piddly rents aren't enough for him. When he looks at this countryside, he doesn't see beauty, or heritage, nature, or livelihoods. He sees green, but it isn't the green of the grass, no. The scoundrel wants to build a resort and golf course for the rich and famous." Conor tucked his thumbs in his pockets. "The only thing holding him back is Dún Castle. Any land he hasn't already gobbled up is yours, Miss Sheridan. And I'm mighty relieved you're here. In another month, I think he'd have convinced the county to declare the place abandoned and auction it off to him at a steal."

"You still live here, though."

"I'm no better than a squatter in the eyes of the law. 'Tis your castle and your land, not mine."

"Hmm." Raegan chewed thoughtfully on her lip.

"Ach! Where are me manners?" Conor smiled big enough to light up the dim hallway. "Let's get to the gallery and the portraits I promised to show ye. Afterward, I'll give you the grand tour. Come on, lad. I assume you can do the driving?"

Raegan chuckled as Drake obligingly pushed her wheelchair behind the old man. Conor O'Malley's flesh might have been weathered and worn, but his spirit was high and warm. Raegan found him to be the kind of person one couldn't help but like.

True to his word, Conor showed Raegan each of her mother's portraits, along with the rest of the family, telling tidbits and anecdotes along the way. She found herself swiping at tears and alternately laughing aloud.

Going to Dun Castle was everything that she'd hoped and none of the things she had feared. It was as if she could feel her mother, the happiness she'd known in that place. Warmth seeped into her chest, a piece of her past that had been missing finally settling into place. She carried that feeling with her through the rest of the tour.

Each room was surprisingly tidy. Most of the furniture was in great shape, though some of the curtains and linens had suffered from dust and moths over the years. Conor assumed responsibility, but Raegan rushed to put a stop to his blaming himself.

"Honestly, everything is in a hundred times better shape than it could be, and I have you to thank for that, Conor. How long has it been empty, anyway?"

Conor scratched his head. "Close to eight years, if memory serves. After your ma left with your pa, your grandmother withered away from grief. Your grandfather, well, he was stubborn as a mule, maybe two. He refused to even hear your ma's name mentioned. He didn't see what it was doing to his wife until it was too late. He shut out the world after that. I brought supplies from town when needed but otherwise didn't bother him. He eventually drank more and ate less until at last a diet of only liquids claimed his life." Conor shook his head. "Foul, evil stuff that rots a man's brains and gives him only the devil for company. I enjoyed a Guinness or three in my younger days, but now, I won't touch the stuff."

Raegan preferred to hide away in books rather than alcohol, so she didn't have much to say, but she thought she caught Drake stiffen out of the corner of her eye. She remembered what he had told her about his own depression and was glad that he'd put down his mug to seek her out for the League. And speaking of them, she directed a new question to Conor. "Did you know my dad, too?"

"Aye. A bit. He used to drop in and talk about the plants with me, even bring me seeds for new flowers and vegetables from time to time. He and your ma, they shared a passion for the land, they did." As he finished talking, they neared the main entrance again. "Well, that's all that I can show ye today. It's high time I go find a bite to eat. Care to join me?"

The mere mention of food made Raegan's stomach grumble. The long walk there and extended tour after had clearly worked up her appetite. "That sounds heavenly," she admitted. "But I don't know that we have the time. It's quite a long walk back to get the rest of our bags. I didn't really expect to find the place so hospitable, so I didn't pack enough to stay the night here."

"Nonsense. There're hours of daylight left, lass. Come break bread with me. Besides, do you really fancy limping your way back over those hills?" Conor strolled off through the courtyard, whistling a merry tune, clearly of no mind to hear refusal.

"He's right," Drake told her. "As long as we eat and don't dawdle, we should make it back to the pub in plenty of time."

"Hello, there," a female voice greeted as Drake rolled Raegan's chair near the gatehouse.

Shauna poked her head in through the big arch. "I see you found the place fine. Oh! Raegan, are you hurt?"

"It's only a slight sprain," Raegan shrugged.

Conor called from the doorway, "Shauna, me beauty. Just in time for supper. Come inside."

And so, their party of four enjoyed a hearty meal of stewed beef and potatoes. By the time the meal had ended, Raegan had been convinced to stay the evening with Shauna while Drake would take a cot at Conor's small home.

"The lad can go and get your bags tomorrow," Conor insisted.

Shauna agreed, hands planted firmly on wide hips. "Right, he can. You want that ankle to heal quicker, then you best stay off of it at least a day."

Seeing that arguments would get her nowhere, Raegan graciously accepted.

18.

Drake knocked on Shauna's door.

No answer.

He tried again, louder.

Still nothing.

His heartbeat ramped up a bit. What if Shauna had left and Raegan had fallen on her weak ankle and gotten hurt? What if she had left? What if…

A screech of laughter broke into his tirade of thoughts. Drake followed the sound around the corner of Shauna's small cottage and found a sight that at first confused him.

Raegan sat on the garden wall, her wrapped ankle stretched out on the stones before her, the other leg swinging over the side. A handful of children bounced up and down around her, some squealing, others asking a million questions all at once.

Only after a second look did he see the book in her hands.

"Good morning," he called, stepping into the middle of the energetic band of children. "What have we here?"

"Miss Raegan?" One of the smallest children pulled her thumb from her mouth. "Is he the ogre?"

"Ogre?" Drake raised an eyebrow.

Raegan stifled a giggle, giving him a once over before she turned back to the little girl. "He may be the ogre, but I believe he is one of the kindest ogres that I've ever met."

"And charming," Drake added. "Don't forget charming."

Raegan rolled her eyes. "Now, where were we?"

A little boy answered. "The ogre was going to swallow Tom Thumb."

"No, Tom was going to kill the ogre," another argued.

Drake lowered himself to the wall and listened as Raegan read to the children, her voice enchanting the words and painting lively scenes before his very eyes. The children, too, were awestruck. They leaned forward, eagerly awaiting the turn of each page. They cheered, they gasped, and at the end of the story, they simply begged for more.

"Tomorrow," Raegan promised.

As they watched the children scamper away to various cottages amongst the hills, Drake couldn't help but smile. He turned to Raegan and was surprised to find her frowning.

"What's with the long look?" he asked. "You had those children eating out of your hand."

"They've never seen one before."

"One what?" Drake asked, brows drawing together in confusion. "An ogre? Come now, surely you haven't seen an ogre either?"

"A book!" Raegan shook the book of fairy tales in front of him and promptly burst into tears.

Drake froze.

Not crying.

Anything but crying.

What was he supposed to do? Drake gently patted her leg, hoping if he got Raegan talking again, maybe the crying would stop.

"I don't understand."

"The children from the village." Raegan rasped out jerky sentences between sniffles. "Their parents live so far from town. The children stay home to help work because rents are so high. They need as much income as they can get. No school. No library. They haven't ever held a book of their own. They've never been read a story and shown pictures and…and…" She buried her head in her hands, shoulders shaking.

Drake rubbed his hand across Raegan's back, offering the most comfort he could.

Shauna found them there five minutes later, and Drake lifted his eyes to her, silently beseeching for help as he shrugged and shook his head.

"Well, what's this now?" Shauna asked. "We get enough rain in these parts without you getting all weepy on my plants."

As if in agreement, the sky opened up, and a light drizzle fell steadily over them all.

"Come on. Into the house with you both."

19.

A few days later, ankle well-mended, Raegan thanked Shauna for her hospitality.

"Are you sure you'll be fine, then?" the kind woman asked over a hearty breakfast.

Raegan laughed. "For the third time, I'm positive. Besides, I'm absolutely dying to explore the castle, and today, I feel well enough to do it. Not even Drake can complain that I haven't taken enough time to rest and heal."

She also knew Drake planned to return to the pub for a few days, so, even if he wanted to harp on her to get extra rest, he wouldn't be around to witness her explorations anyway. The thought made her both excited and sad. She looked forward to spending time alone in the home of her family, but she was keenly aware of the fact that she'd begun to anticipate seeing Drake each day and would miss him.

"If you're sure, then at least let me pack you up a basket of food to take." Shauna began gathering remnants of ham and potato cakes.

Armed with her food and a sense of adventure, Raegan departed with a hug not long after. The air was brisk but Raegan enjoyed every step of her walk, even more so after days filled with lounging and keeping her foot elevated. Nessa trotted along beside her, wandering after a butterfly now and then. The kitten stayed much nearer after her big adventure the day they arrived, and Raegan was glad she didn't have to worry so much about losing her anymore.

As she drew close, Raegan wasn't at all surprised to see Conor waiting for her at the great arch in the wall. He and Drake had been frequent visitors to Shauna's small cottage.

"Good morning," Raegan smiled.

"Morning, lass." He tipped his hat. "Saw ye comin' and lit some fires in the castle this morning."

"That sounds just heavenly!" Raegan gave the old man a quick hug on impulse. "I'm just going to explore a bit today. Maybe tidy up a little and make a pile of linens to wash. I appreciate all of the work you've done to keep this place in good shape. Now it's my turn to get busy."

"You'll find a squat little laundry room around the back, connected off one of the kitchens. I'll say that for the family. They did go in for modern updates over the years, even added my own little bathroom when they put plumbing in." Conor grinned. "The place I worked before settling here still had an outhouse, and I must say, I appreciate not having to run through the rain to take care of business at my age."

Raegan laughed all the way to the castle. Inside, she stood in the hallway, chewing her lip. *Where to explore first,* she wondered. A faint glow at the end of the hallway drew her attention, and she found herself moving toward it. She passed several rooms without a glance. At the hall's end, she turned left after the glow and was surprised to find it further away than she expected. Orange with a hint of green at the edges, it danced and shimmied as she drew close, disappearing at last into a room on the right. Perplexed, she entered the room.

"Oh!" Raegan paused in surprise at the vaulted glass ceiling. The addition of two walls of floor-to-ceiling windows created a cozy conservatory, complete with stunning views of the sea lapping at the shore. The view took her breath away. There were no plants at that time, only plant stands and pots scattered haphazardly around the room. Amongst those, Raegan saw four unique statues of green-garbed little men.

She stepped closer, admiring the lifelikeness of the statues.

"Top of the mornin'." One of the little men inclined his head with a cheeky grin.

"Aigrh!" Raegan gave a strangled cry, leaping backward.

"Now, what kind of greeting is that, lass?" He tapped his cane. "After all, we're practically family."

Raegan caught her breath and studied the men. "Don't tell me—the League of Leprechauns that Drake mentioned?"

"In the flesh." The youngest man with flaming hair smiled. Truly flaming.

Raegan stared in wonder, not at all sure how his head didn't blister under the dancing red-orange flames.

The man with the cane hopped up, surprisingly spry for his appearance, and made introductions. "I'm Ronan. This is Aiden, Oran, and Brandon."

Raegan looked from the first man to each in turn as he told her their names. She tried to find a way to tell the three bearded men apart. Aiden, with his fiery hair, would be easy. When Oran spoke, she knew she would never forget him, either. His voice was beautiful. There was no other way to describe it.

"A pleasure," he said.

Two small words. Yet they floated around the room, lilting and sweet, conjuring images of butterflies, rainbows, and bright smiles in her mind. His voice was made to tell stories.

The last man gave a simple bow, and Raegan decided he must be a man more apt to think than to speak. Nessa, she noticed, wound her way around his feet, purring. The man gave the kitten a small grin.

She turned back to Ronan with a smile. "I'm Raegan. But then, I'm guessing you already know that."

"Aye. Know it we do. Pleased to meet you we are." Aiden grinned.

Ronan turned serious eyes on Aiden, and the fiery-haired man's grin faded as he sat back down on an overturned pot. "Good you've come, it is. The people need you." Ronan's somber eyes matched his grave tone.

"I don't understand." Raegan sighed, running a hand through her hair. "Drake said you mentioned a village to save. Were you talking about this village? It looks perfectly fine. Beautiful, in fact, with sweet people."

"On the surface, yes. But beyond?" Ronan regarded her carefully, fingers tapping gently on his cane.

Raegan frowned thoughtfully. "Do you mean Lord Donovan and his treatment of his tenants?" She began to pace. "I don't really see how I can do anything about that. Even if I stayed here," she rounded on the leprechauns and held up a finger, "which I'm not sure about yet, that won't change how he treats people. He might even decide to develop his resort on a smaller piece of land and move forward anyway." She shrugged.

"Not sure if you're staying, you say." Ronan eyed her. "Tell me, lass, what do you see when you walk this little village? When you admire the view from this castle?"

Raegan crossed her arms. "Beauty. Nature. Wild plants and animals. Bright colors. An untamable sea and rugged coast. Quaint cottages and people."

"Aye. It is all those things." Ronan nodded. "But now close your eyes. Tell me, what does it make you feel?"

Raegan closed her eyes. She could almost feel the salty breeze, the mist in the air. Her memories transported her back to that first glimpse over the hilltop at her home below.

Home.

That was what she felt.

"Home," she answered. "Full. Blessed. Connected. Those are the things I feel," she admitted to herself, as well as to Ronan and the others. "A piece of my heart is still with Evie and Lorcan and my library, but I feel my parents here, and I feel content." She rubbed her forehead in frustration. "So, yes, to your point, I would hate to see any part of this village paved over. That still doesn't help matters. It isn't like I have a say over what happens to the land."

"You could." Brandon spoke for the first time, the soft sound barely more than a hum.

"But how?" Raegan cried in frustration, throwing her arms out. "I'm just—me!"

Ronan smiled, a small sad smile. "Wish we could tell ye, I do, but that is not the way of things. Listen closely, lass. Mayhap Oran can help you find the right path."

Oran sat and pulled a pipe from beneath his hat. "The story of your father and mother, the one you want to know, that story must wait."

Raegan's jaw dropped. Had he read her mind? Before she could ask a thing, Oran continued.

"For now, listen to the tale of the leprechaun king and his fate."

If Raegan had thought Oran's voice beautiful and musical before, it was nothing compared to the tranquil notes and sweet melody that came to life as he began to sing the tale. Nessa trotted over and lay at her feet as they listened together.

"The leprechaun king,

Kind was he,

Friend of man

And healer of the land.

The leprechaun king

Ruled for years on end;

Never met a being who wasn't a friend.

The leprechaun king

Spread good fortune far and wide,

But as time passed so many of his friends died.

The leprechaun king,

With treasure so high,

Ached with emptiness inside.

The leprechaun king

Traveled here and there,

Happened one day upon a maid so fair.

The leprechaun king

Felt his heart come alive

And vowed the maid to be his wife.

The leprechaun king

Begot an enemy then.

The maid's father refused him his daughter's hand.

The leprechaun king

The beautiful maid did love in
return.

She married him, her father's rath
she earned.

The leprechaun king

Set his magic free

For love, mortal he chose to be.

The leprechaun king,

His vast treasure he hid away

In hopes with his wife to return some
day.

The leprechaun king

Said goodbye to his land,

Sailing away, he and his wife hand in
hand.

The leprechaun king

From then on seen no more

Left behind a daughter, the treasure to restore."

As the tune floated away, Raegan blinked and sputtered. "Are you saying the leprechaun king was my father? Seriously? King?"

Brandon flicked his wrist, and a scrap of parchment floated to the floor at her feet. An odd green swirl of smoke rose from Oran's pipe as she bent to retrieve the paper. When Raegan stood up, the little men were gone.

20.

Have you ever heard of a leprechaun king?" Raegan swept a strand of hair from her eyes as she and Conor stood outside the castle, watching the sea. After several hours distractedly cleaning up inside, which mostly involved stripping linens and curtains and throwing them into hallways, then wrestling Nessa out of them before moving to the next room, Raegan had asked Conor for a tour of the grounds. It would do her and Nessa both some good to get some fresh air.

"Can't say as I've heard of one, no. Why do you ask?" Conor tucked his thumbs into his pockets, smiling as usual.

"No reason," Raegan shrugged. She wished Drake were there. She could tell him what the League had said. At least they could get a laugh out of her being called a leprechaun princess together. She couldn't quite bring herself to tell Conor something that sounded so absurd, though.

As they walked on around the back corner of the house, she fingered the folded piece of paper in her pocket. The paper Brandon left for her held the lines of Oran's song on one side, for which Raegan was infinitely grateful. Trying to commit something so lengthy to memory after hearing it only once would have been difficult. On the other side was a short line written in that odd vernacular that the leprechauns spoke. She was having difficulty working out the riddle.

"This is a small garden I've been using for myself." Conor's voice intruded upon her thoughts. "If you're interested, we could expand it in the fall. There's plenty of good ground, and you could plant a number of foods. Might save you some trips into the village to the market."

"Mm-hmm." Raegan nodded assent, working hard to pay more attention. "What's growing now?"

Conor chuckled. "Potatoes, mostly, I'm a good Irishman after all. A few greens, as well."

Raegan laughed and made a mental note to visit the market and see what they had to offer. "I guess it is a good thing I'm rather fond of potatoes myself, then."

Nessa stalked a dragonfly through the neatly laid out rows of vegetables. Raegan feared the kitten would mess up Conor's garden, but when he let out a loud laugh at the kitten's failed attempt to catch her prey, Raegan let her be.

"We've seen the old outhouse, what used to be a kitchen garden, the family cemetery," Raegan paused, sad once more that her mother wasn't there with her family where she belonged. She would have to see that she brought her ashes over and perhaps added them to the little plot somehow, or released them into the ocean behind the castle. She swallowed. "And your lovely garden here. Is there anything else to see?"

Conor grinned, an infectious grin full of life and, if she had to guess, just a little mischief. "As a matter o' fact, there is one more thing. I've been saving the best for last." Picking up Nessa, the old man sauntered away, humming to himself.

Raegan rolled her eyes good-naturedly and followed him around yet another corner of the castle's stone walls. That time, he led her in the direction of the outer perimeter wall toward the ocean, judging by the sound of crashing waves growing louder. When Conor came to a stop a few steps from the wall, Raegan frowned. She didn't see anything but more wall and a few bushes. While the bushes were large, she didn't see anything special about them.

"Here we are," Conor handed over Nessa. "Best hold on to the little tike."

"Okay." Raegan agreed, still confused.

As she rubbed between Nessa's ears, earning a satisfied purr, Conor plucked one of the bushes up and moved it aside to reveal a hole, waist-high, in the wall. Raegan gaped in surprise.

Conor cackled at the expression on her face. "Fake bush," he wiggled it. "Your mother like to sit just outside this wall and watch the waves, but she knew she needed to be able to get back in quickly if your grandfather was looking for her. She enlisted my help in acquiring the bush, but she worked diligently as a girl to carve out her little hideaway all by herself."

Raegan knelt down in the dirt and poked her head through to the other side. "What are these growing out here?" she asked, looking at the forlorn and straggly plants on one side of the hole.

"Well now, let me see." Conor waited for her to move and then peered out. "I'll be! Wild roses. They'll be a beauty when they bloom, if they survive. Looks like they could use a little tending."

"I'll take care of them," Raegan decided. That spot, her mother's spot, would be another way to connect with her. She would care for the plants as she imagined her mother had done. "Thank you for showing me."

"Of course, lass. If truth be told, I think this is where your father and she met." He carefully replaced the fake bush. "I don't know for a fact, now, but I can remember seeing her come back in one night, and her face, it was positively glowing with happy. The stars couldn't have shined brighter that night."

Raegan smirked. She never would have guessed her parents had such an intriguing story. She wished they were there to tell it. Instead, she'd just have to find a way to make Oran tell her sometime.

"Well," Conor dusted his hands off. "I'd best be back to work. Let me know if you need anything." Tipping his hat, he left her in her thoughts and returned to the front of the castle.

Raegan waited until they'd ventured away from the hole in the wall to put Nessa down. Then, she pulled the scrap of paper from her front pocket and reread it as she wandered aimlessly after her exploring kitten.

A treasure of the heart is a treasure in the hands, blessed by the leprechaun king, only to be found by one who wields the magic for the lands.

Raegan didn't wield an ounce of magic that she knew of. Green smoke didn't arise on command, her voice was more akin to a squeaky wheel than a mystical tune if she chose to sing, and she couldn't read minds. She decided to ignore the magic references and focus on the first half of the puzzle. Perhaps if she could find the heart of the castle, she thought excitedly, there would be another secret door or tunnel to the treasure. Her parents did seem to have an affinity for hidden entrances, after all, she thought with a rueful grin.

"Nessa," she called. "Let's get back inside!"

Raegan started in what she figured to be the centermost point of the castle—the dining hall. She ripped dustcovers off of the table and chairs, adding them to the growing pile of laundry, then inspected each table leaf for inscriptions or secret drawers. She carefully turned all of the heavy, thick wooden chairs upside down in the hopes that she would find something secured to the bottoms. She crawled beneath the long bench on one side of the table, collecting nothing but cobwebs and dust bunnies for her efforts. Her meticulous search extended to running her fingertips along all of the nooks and crannies in the walls, tapping her foot every six inches on the stone floor, and generally wishing to find something, anything, that would help her figure out how the League expected her to save the village.

Nothing.

Undeterred, she turned her eyes upward to a large candelabra chandelier that predated when electricity had been added to the castle. She climbed up onto the table and reached, but it was no good. She couldn't touch even the lowest branch.

21.

Drake quickened his steps. Dún Castle was in sight, and he couldn't wait to return.

Though he'd planned to be gone longer, everything at the pub was in order. His barkeep was perfectly capable of managing without him, and the patrons had all been on decent behavior. A few arguments, but no violence. With things running smoothly, Drake didn't see any reason to stick around after a day and a night. On top of that, he didn't want to. The pub had lost its appeal since he'd stopped drinking.

As he walked briskly down the long hill, Drake felt droplets of rain splash onto his arms and head. Soon, the droplets turned into lashings as the skies opened up and released a downpour. Almost to one of the abandoned cabins, Drake jogged off the path and across a field to take shelter inside.

Drake slammed the door shut behind him and turned to survey the front room. A table and chairs sat in a corner, and other than one small leak in the roof, the place was dry. Much to his disappointment, the fireplace yawned, empty of wood and kindling. He pulled out a chair and sat with a sigh. He'd left at dawn that morning. A small nap as he waited would be just the thing, he decided, as he kicked his boots off and rested his feet on the tabletop.

22.

For the second day in a row, Raegan combed the castle, looking for hiding spots. Nessa pounced on her feet as she crawled around her third fireplace, looking for movable bricks or fire-poker handles. Maybe thinking of fireplaces as the heart of a room was a bit of a stretch, but that silly riddle was driving her crazy.

She rocked back on her heels and scooped up the little ball of energy. "What are you complaining about? You've had nothing but playtime all day." She smiled at the purr of her sweet kitten as she rubbed her ears and neck. Nessa stretched, arching her back toward Raegan's hand.

A commotion drew Raegan's attention. A loud bang echoed from the front hallway, followed by yelling.

"I told you, you aren't welcome here. Get out."

Raegan recognized Conor's voice and frowned.

"Move, old man!" Lord Donovan's voice rang out. There was a thud. "Tie him up," Lord Donovan barked.

Raegan froze. The sound of angry footsteps thumped their way closer.

Should she hide? Run? Before she could make up her mind, Nessa meowed in discomfort at her tightening grip.

"Well, well, well." Lord Donovan's icy voice sent shivers down Raegan's spine. Nessa slipped from her hands and scampered away to swat at some dust beneath the kitchen table.

Raegan stood and inched closer to the fireplace. "Where is Conor?" she forced her voice not to quiver.

"He's having a little lie down. The old fool shouldn't have gotten in my way." Lord Donovan placed both hands on his hips. "I presume you've had time to consider my generous offer?"

"Your offer?" Raegan glared. "You mean your threats? I'm not selling you anything." She hoped Conor was okay. She had to get out of there and check on him.

Lord Donovan's lips tightened as he sneered. Clenched fists raised, he advanced, and Raegan found herself stumbling backward. She bumped into the wire basket of fireplace tools. On instinct, she snatched one up.

"What do you plan to do with that tiny shovel?" Lord Donovan laughed.

"Whatever I have to," Raegan whispered. Another set of footsteps echoed through the stone castle. Raegan's heart sped up. Conor, she wondered?

The man who came through the door was neither Conor nor Drake, nor any other soul that she recognized.

"Is it done?"

Raegan gulped as the brawny man nodded to Lord Donovan. "He won't be getting out of that anytime soon."

"Make sure no one else is here," Lord Donovan told the man.

Relief flooded Raegan as she watched the second man leaving the room. Getting away from Lord Donovan would have been hard enough, but she doubted she had a chance if the odds were two against one. Now, she just needed a plan.

Of all the days to choose not to wear her hair clip.

"Now, where we?" the slimy man asked, beady eyes narrowing.

"You were about to leave my property and never come back."

Lord Donovan lifted a finger to his chin as if to consider. "No," he said. "No, that wasn't it. Ah! I remember. I was about to tragically discover that you'd fallen and hit your head on the fireplace, bleeding out with no one to help you."

He smiled, a sick, twisted smile, looking so pleased with himself. The thought flashed through Raegan's mind that if she escaped, she would have nightmares of that look for a long time.

23.

Drake awoke to a crackling sound. He glanced around blearily and caught sight of a fire glowing in the fireplace. He blinked again, realizing no kindling or wood burned, only the fire itself with an odd green tint at the edges.

"Rise and shine, sonny."

Drake groaned. He knew that flippant voice. Sure enough, he looked over and saw Aiden just behind him. "What are you doing here? And where are the other musketeers?"

Aiden didn't even smirk. His face was serious. Even his hair had gone still, Drake noticed with unease, coming swiftly to his feet.

"The other's respect the old ways. They do not get involved." Aiden moved to look out the window.

"Involved in what?"

"The lass is in danger," Aiden spoke. "You must go. Now."

Drake didn't bother with questions or farewells. He rushed from the cabin, headlong into the rain which fell in thick curtains.

Raegan.

He had to get to Raegan.

24.

Raegan swung the fireplace shovel as hard as she could.

It glanced off Lord Donovan's arm as it raised to block it.

She lifted it again, but Donovan jerked it from her hand mid-swing and flung the shovel into a corner.

Retreating, Raegan felt a slight shift in the floor as her foot came down on the stone where the fireplace tools had stood not long before. A grating sound echoed through the room, causing both her and Donovan to look over. Before her eyes, the fireplace swung forward to reveal a dark entrance behind it.

Raegan rushed for it. Pain screamed through her head as Donovan grabbed her ponytail and jerked her backward. She stumbled and fell. Footsteps banged their way into her throbbing head. Bracing for the worst, she turned and nearly sobbed.

Drake!

Drake was there.

25.

Drake watched Donovan jerk Raegan's hair, the snap of her head, her crash to the floor. A primal growl ripped from his throat.

"I'm okay," she shouted. "But Donovan is getting away."

With a curt nod, Drake called on all his willpower to dash past her and after the scum that had just disappeared into what looked like a secret passageway. Blood pumping, adrenaline racing, he took the short flight of stairs two at a time.

The stairs opened into the mouth of a small, low-ceiling room, and Drake very nearly had to duck.

"Donovan, it's over. I found Conor. He's calling the Garda. Come out with your hands up." His training pulsed through him, forsaken but not forgotten. He listened in the stillness and heard heavy breathing just in time. Dodging, he spun around and caught Donovan's wrist, shaking loose the wine bottle that had been about to crash into his head. One quick twist and he had the man's arm pinned behind his back. He shoved him against the wall, perhaps with a little more force than necessary, and growled a whisper of warning into the man's ear that he wouldn't have been free to say if he were still in uniform. Donovan stilled at the threat, and Drake allowed himself a satisfied grin.

"Raegan," he hollered up the stairs. "Find me something to tie him with."

"This should do it." Conor limped down the stairs with Raegan's help, his voice a bit scratchier than normal. He spit on Lord Donovan's shoe and let out a string of Irish so eloquently vile that Drake found himself concealing a laugh. Conor ended with a quick, "Pardon me, lass," to Raegan before handing over the rope and hobbling back up the stairs by himself. "I'll keep an eye out for the Garda," he called over his shoulder.

"What about the second man?" Raegan asked Drake after Donovan was bound, hands and ankles together, and stuffed against the wall to wait. For good measure, she'd sacrificed her socks to make a gag to silence the sputtering rage spewing from the terrible man's mouth.

"He is locked in Conor's gatehouse. He tried to escape, but Conor shoved a wheelbarrow in front of him. Tripped and hit his head, so we wheeled him into the house and blocked the door from the outside." Drake spoke quietly, all the while drawing closer to Raegan. She hadn't said much, but he'd seen her trembling before he chased after Lord Donovan. He took her hand and looked into her eyes, brushing a red curl behind her ear.

If he'd been one moment later…

Drake closed his eyes and pulled her into a fierce kiss, trying to banish the thought, the fear.

26.

Raegan walked barefoot on the earthen floor, hands trailing across dusty shelves, most empty, a few boasting bottles of wine, bags of potatoes, or kegs.

She asked one of several questions on her mind and turned as Drake explained how he and Conor had restrained Lord Donovan's thug. He walked slowly to her, eyes never leaving her own as he talked. She found it hard to concentrate on what he was saying. All she could think was how happy she was that he was there, how relived that he had come to her rescue, how she wanted to keep him all to herself.

So immersed in her own thoughts was she that Raegan didn't even realize

Drake was pulling her closer until suddenly his lips met hers. She was lost. Relief, passion, fear, joy, they all mingled together until she was dizzy.

A throat clearing severed the moment, and Raegan pulled away. She looked up the stairs and saw Conor grinning ear to ear.

"The Garda are here," he informed them.

Sure enough, two officers soon appeared at the top of the stairs and made their way down. Drake and Raegan gave brief statements, agreeing to make the journey to the station the next day to go over all of the details and sign them.

Shauna, having noted all of the activity from her cottage, appeared as the men were hauling Lord Donovan and his man away. With eagle eyes, she took note of Conor's limp and swooped in to fuss over him, even as she chastised him for being up and about.

"You are not doing one more thing today," Shauna scolded. "You are going inside to rest and eat something besides a potato. I'll make sure of it myself."

As Shauna led him away, Conor peeked over his shoulder at Raegan and Drake and gave a wink. It was all Raegan could do to smother a laugh.

Alone with Drake again, Raegan grew nervous. To cover it, she asked about the pub and his trip.

"Nothing out of the ordinary," Drake shrugged. "I'd rather talk about you. You nearly gave me a heart attack, you know."

"Excuse me!" Raegan said, striking an offended pose. "It isn't like I invited that vile man here to attack me. I can't help it if you leave right before all of the visitors begin to drop in around here."

"Visitors?" Drake ran a hand through his dark, messy hair. "I'm afraid to even ask who else could have possibly come by."

"I'll give you one guess," Raegan smiled. "No, make that four little guesses."

"The League of Leprechauns showed up? When?"

Raegan explained about the appearance of the men and then showed Drake the paper with the ballad and the riddle. "I've been searching and searching," she admitted. "But I haven't found a thing. I don't even know what I'm searching for. Seriously, do I think a pot of gold is just going to be waiting somewhere?" She rubbed her neck, shrugging. "It was silly."

"It isn't silly." Drake held her hand and led her back into the castle. "You should have waited for help, though. I don't think I'll ever be able to leave you alone in this place again."

"I don't think I want you to," Raegan admitted with a small smile. She blushed as Drake gave her a firm peck on the cheek.

"What have you got to eat in this place?" Drake asked. "Being the dashing hero is hard work on a man's appetite, you know."

After a snack of corned beef sandwiches, Drake cleared the table, and Raegan washed the dishes. "Do you have any other ideas about the riddle?" he asked her.

Raegan, drying her hands on a towel, leaned against the cabinet. She tilted her head and considered the words again, repeating them in her head.

A treasure of the heart is a treasure in the hands, blessed by the leprechaun king only to be found by one who wields the magic for the lands.

"I guess it would help if I knew something more about my mom's past, something she treasured…" Raegan sprang forward. "Wait, there *is* one more place that I didn't think to look. It's a long shot, but heck, so were all the others."

"Lead the way," Drake said.

*   *   *

Raegan lay one of the shovels they'd found in the tool shed aside and sagged against the stone wall, staring out at the sunset reflecting on the dark sea.

Her heart skipped a beat as Drake's shovel clanged against something hard. They kneeled and moved aside more dirt by hand.

"Ugh!" Raegan groaned. "Another rock." She tossed it in the growing pile nearby. "I really thought I'd figured it out this time," she sighed. "Conor showed me this place and said it was one of my mother's special, secret places to come. If she kept it private, surely she treasured it. Oh well, I guess I should give up."

"You don't seem the giving up sort," Drake said. "But I think taking a break is okay."

Raegan nodded. "Maybe you're right. Let's get these rosebushes back in the ground before we do some real harm."

Together, they carefully unwrapped the roots and replanted the bushes against the outer wall. Drake moved to collect the shovels. Raegan was smoothing the last of the dirt in place when he tapped her on the shoulder.

"Hmm?" she asked without looking up.

"I think you should see this."

Raegan wiped her dirty hands on her jeans and rose, her head turning to follow Drake's pointing finger. She gasped. "You've got to be kidding me. Is that what I think it is?"

Just above the shoreline, two pieces of the cliff stuck out, creating a heart-shaped overhang only visible as the sun's last rays shined perfectly through its center.

Drake held out a shovel. "What do you say? One more treasure hunt?"

Raegan grinned, scrambling over the dirt and rocks like a kid. "I'll race you," she called over her shoulder.

"Blasted woman," Drake growled. "You're going to hurt your ankle again. Slow down!"

"That sounds like someone who is losing trying to stop the winner," Raegan teased.

Slipping and sliding, they made it to the beach without injury. Raegan slowed to catch her breath. Her gaze lit on two tiny carvings as she came abreast of the rocks.

Initials.

She traced over them, tears springing to her eyes.

"This is it," she whispered.

Drake placed a hand on her shoulder. "What is?"

"These are my parents initials." She pointed. "This is it. The treasure of the heart. Each other. This place. This land."

"After you." Drake inclined his head to the soft earth beneath their feet, damp but shielded from the waves by all of the rocks.

Raegan barely heard him. She laid her shovel down, moving along the rocks, past the initials. There, beneath the moss, she caught site of another carving. A shamrock.

"Look!" She squealed.

Drake stooped. "Is that another one?"

Sure enough, a trail of mostly hidden, lightly-carved shamrocks led to a large boulder. Drake tried to move it; the rock didn't budge.

Raegan nudged him aside. "I think I need to get behind it." She pointed to a small crevice, too small for Drake, but if she turned just right, Raegan could fit.

"I don't know," Drake frowned.

Raegan was already squeezing through the opening, heedless of anything but the possibility of finding her father's treasure.

Drake's voice grew muffled. The sounds of the waves softened. As her eyes adjusted to the dimness, she realized she was in a cave of sorts. It was so short that she had to crawl. The floor was damp stone and rough on her hands and knees. Nessa, the rotten kitten, rubbed against her shin and made her jump. She prayed under her breath not to find any snakes or other creepy, crawly creatures taking refuge in the place.

As she felt along the floor and walls for anything loose, a dim glow began in the corner, only five or six feet back. Rather than frightened, Raegan grew excited. That glow looked suspiciously similar to the green smoke that had come from the leprechaun's pipe.

Raegan crawled toward it, wincing at the gravel bits digging into her skin, eager to discover what her father had hidden away that the League felt so certain would help her save the village.

27.

R aegan? Raegan can you hear me?"
Drake called again. He knelt in the
wet sand, peering into the hole
through which Raegan had disappeared.

"I'm here," Raegan answered, her
face appearing before him at last.

Drake scrubbed a hand over his face.
"Why is it you're determined to give me a
heart attack?" he asked ruefully.

Raegan grinned and then sobered. "I
have a question for you."

"Okay?"

"How much money is a pound of
gold worth?"

Drake thought. "Not sure, but I'd say around fifteen hundred euros would be close based on the last time I saw a currency table."

As he watched Raegan chew thoughtfully on her lower lip, he reached a hand into the cave and tilted her chin up. "Come on. It's okay if the treasure isn't much. You already helped the people of the village by getting rid of Donovan."

"Oh! It isn't that," Raegan laughed. She scooted aside and pointed to the back corner of the cave.

Drake followed her finger, eyes widening in shock at the mound of gold blocks surrounded by a faint green glow.

"I was trying to do the math on maybe one or two hundred pounds to euros." Lying on her elbows, she clapped her hands together, her face radiant with glee. "I think the League was right. I'll be able to save this village not just from Donovan, but from anyone who wants to uproot the people for financial gain ever again." She waggled her eyebrows. "Plus, I'd say there will be enough left over for a very special project that I have in mind."

Drake tried to ferret the information out of her, but Raegan insisted on keeping her project a secret until she was certain she would be able to do it. The onery woman not only refused to tell him, but she extracted a promise that he would help her with whatever in the world she had planned.

Drake smiled. *Not that it had been a difficult promise to make*, he thought, as he slipped his hand into hers. They hurried back to the castle to retrieve bags to carry the gold out with. Dark was fast approaching, and though the gold had been fine for decades, Raegan was like a little kid at Christmas. She couldn't wait a second longer to put her plans for the village into action. They would leave at first light with the gold and head to a solicitor in the village that could assist them with the legal side of things.

28.

Raegan thrummed her fingers nervously in her lap, afraid that at any minute the solicitor would demand to know where the gold came from, accuse her of stealing, tell her that the Wyndham's Land Purchase Acts didn't apply there, or really any number of things, none of which happened.

Two hours after she and Drake entered the small office rooms above the post office, they walked out with Raegan holding the deeds to every property within a two-hundred-mile radius of Dún Castle. She'd bought out Donovan's leases as he sat in a holding cell, awaiting trial where bail was rumored to be set at an astronomical amount. Apparently, any money looked like good money, and he hadn't put up a fight.

Of course, the fact that Raegan insisted the solicitor keep her name as facilitator of the purchase anonymous had probably helped smooth the way.

She practically floated down the sidewalk. Only one thing provided a dim spot in her bright plan. Spotting a pay phone, she asked Drake to give her a moment.

"Evie?" she said with relief when her friend answered on the second ring. "It's Raegan."

"God bless you, child! I'm so happy to hear from you. How has your trip been?"

Raegan took a deep breath. That part wasn't going to be easy. "It's so beautiful here. The trip has been wonderful. The castle is like nothing I imagined. It has all been rather better than I ever expected, except for one or two small incidents."

"I knew it. I knew you would be getting into trouble over there." Evie's worry carried clearly through the line. "Are you okay? What's happened?"

"I'm fine," Raegan assured.
"Everything worked out. There's something else I need to tell you though." Closing her eyes, she braced herself for an argument. "I've decided to move here, to Dún Castle, my mother's home. The village…it's hard to explain…but I think that I can help the people here. Oh Evie, the children!" The words came tumbling out as she told Evie about the people she'd met, the friends, the enemy she'd found in Lord Donovan. She even admitted to finding her father's treasure, though quietly. She didn't need to create new enemies so soon, after all.

"Well, of course you're going to stay."

Raegan nearly dropped the phone in shock. "What?"

Evie chuckled. "Dearie, I watched you and that handsome fellow walk away, and I knew you weren't coming back. I don't blame you. That's why I've had my bag packed since the day after you left."

"Your bag?"

"Of course! A castle sounds like a big place. You'll be needing someone to help and, goodness knows, cook." Evie paused. "What about the library?"

"Leave everything to me," Raegan said, smiling as she ended the call.

Evie was coming. There was just Lorcan and Joan to break the news to.

Ten minutes later, she walked back to Drake, shaking her head.

He raised one eyebrow. "You look like the cat who ate the canary."

"Is it that obvious?"

Drake laughed. "Just tell me the good news before you burst wide open."

"They're all coming!" Raegan clasped her hands to her mouth, still unable to believe her good fortune. Or, more accurately, her good family. "Evie, Lorcan, Joan, they're all moving to Ireland, to the village. Joan said it sounded like a fairy tale, and she was more than happy to jump right in. Lorcan…well…I think Lorcan has always wanted to come back, but he felt an obligation to me after my father's death. He's already talking about opening a pub here."

"I think I've got just the place for him. My pub could use more good cooking and less drinking idiots." Drake smiled. "And Evie?" he asked.

"She's got to come and help with the castle, of course." Raegan winked.

Drake groaned. "What you mean is that woman plans to keep an eye on me and likely work me to death to make sure that you're well taken care of."

"Of course! What else could I mean?" Raegan smiled smugly.

"You and this family of yours are going to be the death of me." Drake grabbed her hand and spun her around in the street.

"But oh, won't it be a wonderful way to go?" Raegan laughed.

"The best." Drake nodded, placing a kiss on her fingers. "Now, let's get home and share the news with Nessa."

"Home." Raegan breathed, closing her eyes. "I like the sound of that."

30.

Drake watched her.

He followed her every move with his eyes.

His wife looked up at him and smiled so big it nearly consumed him. Though it had been six months since they married, Drake couldn't believe how blessed he was to have Raegan as a wife, a partner.

She sat on a large blanket in the courtyard, fifteen of the village children spread out around her, hanging on her every word. As the story she read came to a close, they all groaned.

"Now, now," Raegan admonished. "That's all I have time to read today if we're going to move on to the surprise that I have for you all."

"Surprise?"

"What surprise?"

Excitement rippled through the group, even the older children having trouble sitting still.

"Come and see." With that, Raegan nudged Nessa out of her lap as she stood and led the way into the large front doors of the castle.

Drake followed, scooping up the tiniest little girl whose short legs couldn't keep up with the others.

"Where are we going?" one of the boys asked.

Raegan stopped in front of a set of double doors. Crouching down, she whispered to the children, "Somewhere magical." With a secret wink for Drake's eyes alone, she threw the doors open and stepped aside.

The children stampeded inside and stopped. Some turned in circles, others stared, and a few of the braver souls took off to one of many shelves and tables overflowing with books.

"What is this place?" Imogen, the oldest in the group at eleven years, asked Raegan softly.

"The most magical place of all—a library," Raegan answered.

"Are you going to read us all these books?" another child wanted to know, holding two in both hands.

Raegan shook her head, and the faces around her dimmed. "No," she said slowly. "I'm going to teach you to read them yourselves. They're all for you."

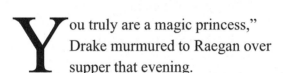

31.

You truly are a magic princess," Drake murmured to Raegan over supper that evening.

Shauna and Conor raised their glasses, clamoring in agreement. Both had been overwhelmed when they learned that Raegan had freed all of the tenants from Lord Donovan as a landlord and made it possible for them to begin buying back their own land.

Just in time, she had remembered the section in the history book she'd read on the journey from England that discussed such matters. The solicitor had been most eager to help her set things right for the people of her village to have a better future.

Raegan blushed and shook her head. She counted her blessings, each of them sitting around the table with her: Lorcan, Joan, Evie, Shauna, Conor, and especially Drake. She looked at the portrait of her mother on the wall and the poem of her father framed beside it.

The leprechaun king.

The thought still made her laugh.

Finally, she smiled. "I'm not magic at all, but I certainly know where to find all of the magic I need." She looked around slowly. "It is in each one of you and in the power of stories in books that bring love, joy, adventure, hope, and healing. This village needed healing, and thanks to each one of you and your support, I think they're well on their way to receiving it.

"Family and hope." Raegan raised her glass for a toast. "Along with the powerful portals to be found in books, of course. Those bits of magic I'll happily wield every day."

She squeezed Drake's hand, pretending not to notice the faint green glow from the hallway or the four nodding heads in the doorway, smiling in approval, before they vanished again.

From the Author

Did you enjoy The Librarian's Treasure?

You can read the prequel story of Raegan's parents free by joining my newsletter at the following web address or scan the QR code.

https://mailchi.mp/54deb94fcbc4/freepreque lforjoiningkbbnewsletter

Prefer not to join? No problem. The prequel will also be available for purchase or free to read with Kindle Unlimited.

Want to try winning your free ebook copy of the prequel story instead? Great! Visit my website for entry rules at http://katherinebrownbooks.com/giveaways/

Other Books by Katherine Brown

Ooey Gooey Bakery Mystery Series:

Rest, Relax, Run for Your Life

Pastries, Pies, & Poison

Bake, Eat, & Be Buried

Savory, Sweet, & Scandalous

Couches & Catastrophes (Book 3.5)

Red Velvet & Romance (Book 4.5) A
Valentine's Short

White Chocolate, Weapons, & a Walk
Down the Aisle (Book 5)

Fairy Tale Retellings (Novelettas)

Marigold and the Bear Necessities

Cloaked

Children's Books

Princess Bethani's First Garden Party

Princess Bethani's Surprise Visitor

Ghost Boy Camps Out

Tiny Princess & the Big Llama Drama

Becky Beats the Mean Girls

Adventures of Gladys (Ooey Gooey Spinoff Series)

Bonbon Voyage

Half-Baked Homecoming

Made in the USA
Middletown, DE
15 April 2022

64305332R00126